# The Chaos Court

## Jake Burnett

SOUTH
WINDOW
PRESS

*To Ruth*

Printed in the United States of America

First Printing, 2020

ISBN 978-1-7346642-0-1

South Window Press
P.O. Box 6573
Raleigh, NC 27628

www.southwindowpress.com

Cover design: Rocío Martín Osuna
Cover concept sketch: Elissa Phillips

# Contents

# 1. The Offaltosser

The day Patience Fell turned twelve, she bid farewell to her family farm.

Her father gave her a firm handshake. "Be kind," he said.

Her mother gave her a brand-new broom. "Work hard."

Her seven brothers and sisters gave her one hug each.

"You'll do fine," her parents said together after the hugging was done. Without further ado, Patience shouldered her little pack, hopped on the back of a turnip wagon, and turned her face to the road.

The Fells were a country family and not given to displays.

She arrived in the town of Whosebourne early the next morning. Her goal was to find her place in the world. Everyone said that was what you did when you turned twelve, and her parents' farm (with all those mouths to feed) didn't have enough room for her.

The wagon driver let her off at the gate market. In return for the ride, she helped him unload the turnips.

"You sure you know what you're doing from here?" he asked when they were done. "Whosebourne's mighty big."

"Yes, sir."

"Fancy houses sometimes put out signs for broomgirls." He climbed back onto his wagon with a grunt. He clucked the old horse into a slow plod. "Inns too. Look for those."

Patience knew that. It had been her plan all along to find just such a place, but she thanked him for the advice anyway. Gripping her broom, she strode off down the street on her mission.

The townsfolk bustled all around her. They jostled past with very serious faces. No one paid Patience much mind—but then, they didn't pay each other much mind either.

Everyone talked all at once, as if everyone else were listening just to them. Iron wheels rattled on the cobblestone streets. Bells rang over the rooftops. A dozen sounds she couldn't identify echoed from every corner. The combined clatter and chatter of Whosebourne made as little sense as the juts and twits of nervous birds in the dark woods back home.

She was passing an inn called *The Crock and Dice* when she heard a muffled voice under the racket. Someone was crying. Patience stopped. The crowd tried to shove her out of its way. She stood her ground, listening to find the source of the sound.

In the alley next to the inn, a girl about her own age slumped all alone on the stoop of a kitchen door. She sobbed into her apron. A bundle of clothes tied to the end of a broom was propped up against the wall next to her.

No one in the street went to check on the girl weeping in the alley. No one even spared her a glance. So Patience pushed against the flow of uncaring townsfolk, till she cleared the crowd and stood by the stoop.

"Do you need help?"

The other girl replied with jagged sobs. Patience put a hand on her shuddering shoulder.

"AH!" The girl jerked her head up. Her eyes were wide as a spooked stallion's. She wasn't looking at Patience though.

Leaning out of the garret window of the inn, three stories up, a woman with ink stains on both cheeks was watching them. She cocked her head to the side. She whistled a curious three-note tune.

"Tu-whit, tu-whoo!" she chirped.

"No!" the girl on the stoop shouted up. "You're all mad and I won't fix it!"

Just then, the wind rose in the alley. A scrap of fish-stained butcher paper danced across the cobblestones.

Several more bits of garbage whirled around Patience's feet.

"Offaltosser!" The girl leapt off the stoop. She seized her broom-and-bindle. She sprinted into the street, muscled through the crowd, and disappeared from view.

That's when things took a turn for the odd.

The bits and scraps and snips of trash blowing around the alley swirled up into a funnel cloud of mess. This whirling thing hovered in front of Patience, twice her height.

"Fox in a bonnet!" she cried. (It was something her mother said when surprised.)

She swiped with her broom at the tumbling pieces of garbage. The funnel jumped back, so she missed by a bristle.

A stream of what sounded like curses burst from the filthy storm. "Schmecktenfrettle! Borging skell and blicking fritch!"

"I don't know what that means," Patience hefted her broom, "but you'd better take it back."

The storm tossed several day-old fish at her, which she nimbly dodged. They struck the door behind her — one, two, three. They stuck there a second, then slid down, leaving stinky, glistening trails of guts and scales.

Patience wrinkled her nose.

"You'll have to throw better than that to hit me."

She stamped her foot. She turned to the side. She squared her hips. She stuck out her chin and took a big swing at the strange whirling thing.

Her broom head connected with a soft melon on an updraft. The fruit flew across the alley and splattered all over the wall of the building next door.

A quivering ball of creamy noodles shot back at her. Patience dropped to the ground. Even so, some curdled noodle-cream splashed down the back of her neck. Seizing the high ground, the whirlwind bore straight down on her. It sputtered the most awful, unrepeatable things. She rolled out of the way, over several nasty lumps of squishy ick. She twisted her legs under her and sprung up. She brandished her broom.

"Oi! Come on then!"

The trash-storm reversed course. It fired a barrage of wet chicken bones as it charged. Patience knocked the bones out of the air one after another. She stepped out of the whirlwind's path. The wind fluttered the hem of her skirt as it passed. She set herself firm. She drew the broom back as far as it would go and whacked the cursing garbage right in its middle as hard as she could.

This time, instead of a piece of trash, she hit something far more solid. The wind stopped cursing mid-curse. Every bit of garbage in the air dropped to the ground. A tiny filthy man, who till that moment had been invisible, appeared where the whirlwind had been. He rolled head over heels across the alley. He bounced off the brick wall of *The Crock and Dice* and fell face down in a puddle of sour milk and mustard.

He lay there and did not move.

"Oh dear!" Patience exclaimed.

She peered at the unpleasant little man. She reached out the bristle-end of the broom as far as it would go, until she could poke him. He did not react. She prodded him again, more firmly. He lay as still as a sack of wet barley. She worked the handle tip underneath him and flipped his limp body over.

"Are you dead?"

She had to laugh when she heard herself say that. Of course he wasn't dead. She hadn't hit him *that* hard.

Still, he wasn't moving. Concerned, she stepped closer. She pulled her collar up over her nose and mouth. He smelled like the largest cowpie ever, steaming all summer day long in the sun, packed down into a space the size of a mangy alley cat.

"Sir? Hello?"

Still nothing. Worrisome. He clearly needed her help. She took as deep a breath as she dared through the sturdy fabric of her dress and bent down to investigate. She heard a faint wheezing sound from his crusty lips.

"Well, that's good," she said with some relief. "Now let's see about getting you inside."

She checked around the alley for something she could use to scrape him off the cobbles without touching him. Before she could do that, he leapt suddenly to his feet. Panic seized his face.

"Dreck and drettle!" He scuttled into a drain pipe and was gone.

Out in the street, the townsfolk kept rushing by. No one seemed to have seen the weird whirlwind fight.

## 2. Crowquill

Fighting an invisible trash-throwing man had not been part of Patience's plan. She stood in the alley, thinking. Should she tell someone about him? She had no idea who.

"Tu-whit, tu-whoo!"

The ink-stained woman in the attic window was still watching her.

"Oi!" Patience called up. "What was that all about?"

The woman cawed three times. A large crow flew down to her window sill. He shook himself so that one tail feather came free. He flew off. The woman snatched the feather out of the air and tucked it into her wild black hair.

She looked Patience straight in the eye. "You cared for the offaltosser! Perhaps you'll do, when the Chaos Court comes for you!"

"Perhaps I'll do? Do what? Offaltosser? The Chaos who? Fox in a bonnet!"

"CAW!" The woman jerked back into her room. She vanished behind a slap of shutters.

Patience was not so easily put off. She was going to find her place in Whosebourne, no doubt. But she wanted to know if the whole town was mad. She wasn't sure what she'd do if it *were*, but the first step was finding out.

She opened the alley door to the inn. In the kitchen beyond, a frazzle-haired woman whose wrinkles had wrinkles looked up from a smoking skillet. She glared at Patience.

"Dawdled long enough over the trash, didn't you, girl?"

"Begging your pard —"

"Hop to! Hop to! I'll be needing you to take the oats to Miss Crow —" The cook stopped. "Wait. You're not Bess."

"No, ma'am," Patience said. "I'm P —"

" — Mags! That was the last one." The cook squinted at her. "But you're not Mags either."

"Ma'am, I'm —"

"What'd you do with Mags?" She emptied the enormous skillet onto several plates. She frowned. "Or was it Ella?"

"She left, ma'am!" Hastily, before the cook could interrupt her again, Patience went on. "She had her broom and a bundle. I don't think she's coming back."

"MISS ALYS!" a chorus of voices shouted from the other room.

"COMING!" the cook bellowed back. She hoisted three big trays of breakfast. "Give me strength. Where'm I going to find another broom-girl?"

Patience saw in an instant this was her chance. She could find a job *and* be able to get some answers from the woman in the attic.

"Ma'am?"

"What, girl? Be quick before that lot out there eats the drapes and starts on the tables!"

Patience took a deep breath. She had a speech prepared, listing all her good qualities and why they meant someone should take her on.

"Is that your broom?" the cook asked before she could start.

"Yes."

"You're hired. Take that tray of oats to Miss Crowquill in the attic and be back down before these doors stop swinging!"

With that, Miss Alys charged into to the common room to feed the raucous crowd.

Proud of herself at having sheared two sheep at the same time, Patience hung her broom on a hook. She stowed her pack under a table. She found a tray of oats, tea, cream, and berries and carefully carried it up the dim-lit servant stairs.

At the top, she found a hatch in the ceiling with a small hook in it. A long stick with a leather loop on one end hung on the wall to Patience's left. She reached for the stick while balancing the tray on one knee. It nearly upended. Milk and tea slopped on the floor.

Being a servant was going to take practice.

She set the tray down. Using the hem of her dress, she sopped up the creamy brown puddle from the floorboards. She took the stick from the wall. Stretching as tall as she could, she hooked the trapdoor to the attic. She tugged. Stairs unfolded into the hall, hitting the floor with a big BAHCLUNK!

She hung the pull-stick in its place and picked up the breakfast tray. She wasn't sure what was proper to do next. Was she supposed to go up? Or wait for the mysterious Miss Crowquill to come down?

Faint chirrups and tu-whoos drifted down from the open hatchway. They weren't welcoming sounds, but they didn't say 'go away' either.

She decided to go up. Nobody ever said no to tea and oats. And nobody got answers by not asking questions.

"In for a lamb, in for the herd," she said, as her father did whenever he was about to do something uncertain. Balancing the breakfast on her head, she stepped up the rickety attic ladder.

Upstairs in the garret, there was not a surface clear to set the tray. Sheaves of paper were strewn over a dozen mismatched pieces of cast-off furniture. All of the pages were covered in large loopy-lettered writing.

Shoved into a far corner of the attic sat a roll-top desk with a broken roll-top. At it hunched Miss Crowquill— the same woman Patience had seen at the window, with the wild hair and the weird way of holding her head. She scribbled with a black feather pen, tossing page after page aside at a furious pace.

"Breakfast, ma'am?" Patience asked, with a little cough (part to get the woman's attention and part because the room was rather dusty).

Crowquill muttered little nonsense words to herself. She scritch-scratched page after page.

Patience spotted another tray, with dirty dinner dishes, atop a bookshelf. Not at all gracefully, she picked up the old tray with one hand while replacing it with the new one. Proud of herself for managing the switch without throwing dishes everywhere, she curtsied to no one in particular.

The weird poet leapt to her feet. She danced to the window with light little steps. She flung it open.

A crow waited on the sill. The woman bent down with a folded piece of paper in her mouth. The bird took it gently in his beak.

"Flutter through the iron of the gate most fair," Crowquill whispered, almost too soft for Patience to hear. "Find my Johnny in the Who-Knows-Where."

The bird nodded and took to wing.

As though this were an entirely ordinary thing, Crowquill closed the window and poured herself a mug of tea.

"Good work with the offaltosser, dear," she said to Patience. She added a dollop of cream. Her hand trembled, as if with nerves. Her head never stood still. In fact, her whole body twitched in an unsettling way. It seemed to Patience that the woman was *afraid* of her. Or excited. Neither made any sense.

"I just whacked some trash, ma'am."

"And out popped the little man and away he ran, away he ran."

Patience wasn't sure what to say. She had had all manner of questions, but Crowquill's strange, twitchy manner had muddled her.

"And you didn't just stay." Crowquill's big dark eyes peered at Patience over the edge of the mug. "You tried to help him out. You *cared*."

"Of course I did. It's just what people do."

"Not true, not true!" Crowquill waved the mug, sending tea raining down on a stack of scratched-out verse. "So far, it's only been you! And maybe, just maybe you'll do!"

She broke into a fit of giggles.

That did it for Patience. Even if she was just a country girl on her first day in town, she wasn't going to be made fun of.

"Oi!"

She slammed the dish tray on the floor with a rattle-and-bang. Crowquill jumped and fluttered her hand over her mouth. Patience folded her arms.

"Maybe I'll do what?"

Crowquill pointed with the trembling cup. "See what my Johnny has to say. That book there."

She snatched up the oat bowl and scurried to her desk.

On top of the bookshelf, Patience saw a large book, bound in brown leather with the title in silver letters.

*THE CHAOS COURT*

*BY JOHNNY FACTOTUM*

She regarded it skeptically.

"An old book? How's this going to tell me anything?"

"Just read," Crowquill mumbled around a sticky mouthful of oats. "I marked the spot."

The book bulged near the middle, where a grilled leek had been inserted as a bookmark.

Patience opened *The Chaos Court*. She peeled the day-old leek off the page. The printing was old-fashioned and some of the words were new to her, so she had to sound them out loud.

*The Offaltosser*

*In Appearance most foul and of Odor quite disgusting, the Offaltosser is among the least fair members of the Chaos Court. When Cities and Towns do slight the Fair Folk, the Chaos King sends a Plague of Offaltossers, who will create a mighty Wind. This smelly Tornado stirs up all the Filth and Trash of the Town, making Life quite unpleasant for Plain Folk. The Offaltosser's Trash Wind is accompanied by Curses and Words of Ill Use that offend the Ears of any goodly Person, as much as the Flinging of Trash offends their Noses. The Sighting of this filthy wee Man and the Hearing of his Curses is therefore said to be most unlucky.*

"I don't see how this helps," Patience said, adding a belated "Ma'am."

"Maybe you haven't read far enough?"

Not believing a word of that, Patience returned to the book.

*However, if One should be kind enough to care even for this foul Fellow –*

"Yes, yes?" Crowquill's voice quivered.

"That's all. The rest of it's covered in leek sauce."

Crowquill scraped the bottom of the bowl with her spoon. "Tuu-what?"

Patience repeated herself.

"Is it?" Crowquill appeared over her shoulder. "Oh no!"

She seized the book from Patience's hands. She licked her thumb and scrubbed at the smudge. That made it worse.

"Sorry, sorry, sorry," she said, over and over, tears in her eyes.

"It's alright, I'm sure, ma'am." Patience was taken aback at how upset Crowquill was over a smudged book. She didn't like seeing anyone cry and hoped she hadn't done anything to cause it. "Really, it's fine. I don't need to read the rest."

"You don't understand," Crowquill sobbed over the ruined page, "It's my only —"

" — GIRL!" Miss Alys shouted up from the floor below. "DOWN HERE NOW!"

"AH!" Crowquill scuttled into her bed. She pulled the covers over her head. A cascade of pages slithered to the floor.

Frowning in a fashion most unbecoming a broom-girl, Patience hurried downstairs, laden with dirty dishes and a dozen unasked questions.

## 3. The Carriage with the Key on the Side

The week that followed, however, left her little time to find answers.

Miss Alys worked Patience hard, teaching her the trade of being a broom-girl. She barely had space to think. On those rare lapses where she spared a moment to wonder about offaltossers or the previous broom-girls, the cook appeared in an instant with a dozen new things to be done.

Miss Alys had a keen nose for wool-gathering and no tolerance for such.

Every day was a blur of work. Every night, Patience dropped into her little bed and fell asleep at once. She didn't have time to dream. Dawn and the breakfast mess came as soon as she closed her eyes.

At the end of Patience's first week, right before the dinner rush, Miss Alys swept breathlessly into the kitchen. The cook snapped her fingers at her.

"Off with your apron," she said. "And clean your face."

Patience hopped up from stirring the gravy to keep it from lumping. "Yes, ma'am."

"No time for yes nor ma'am. Wash, wash, wash!"

While Patience scrubbed her greasy cheeks, Miss Alys talked at her — a rushing stream of confusing commands.

"Don't act too country. Be on your best behavior. No, that won't do. Be on *my* best behavior."

"What is —"

" — curtsy when you're thinking what to say. No! Don't say anything. Listen. Till they tell you what to say. Then say that."

"Who —"

" — say please and thank you and always put sir or ma'am in the front and back. Like two pieces of bread round what you say. The Servant Sandwich, it's called. Can you remember that?"

"The Servant Sandw —"

" — ich, yes. Now, off with that apron."

"Ye—oof!" The cook yanked the apron off over her head without bother to untie it.

"And don't grunt like a flopping sow."

Patience rubbed her ears, which the apron string had nearly taken off. "Whagoinon?" she said as one quick word, hoping not to be interrupted.

Miss Alys spit on her thumb. She scuffed Patience's cheek—which was perfectly clean.

"Oi!"

"None of that!" Miss Alys herded her into the alley with little swats of the apron.

A one-horse fly carriage waited in the street; a large black key on a white background was painted on its side. The alley was otherwise empty. Patience wished she had her broom, in case another offaltosser showed up. This was an odd turn of events and anything could happen next.

Instead of a trash storm, a normal, ordinary man came round the corner. Perhaps not quite ordinary. He wore a very fine red coat with a silver key on the lapel and black velvet trousers. His black boots gleamed. His ginger whiskers were trimmed pristine. He was fancier than anyone Patience had ever seen.

Mister Jankyn, the innkeeper, followed a step behind. He rubbed his hands together like he was washing them something fierce. He smiled a toothy and too-big grin (the one Patience had noticed he only put on for the best-paying customers. He pointed at her.

"Sir, there's our girl, sir," he said in a booming fake voice. "Miss Prudence Tumble!"

"It's Patience Fell!" she objected.

Miss Alys nudged her with a knee.

"It's not a difficult name," she muttered to the cook. "And I've been here a week."

Miss Alys cleared her throat unnecessarily loudly. Patience knew well the look on her face—her mother made the same face when argument was a sure key to a whipping. So she gave up. She even threw in a curtsy.

"Sir, sorry, sir."

Judging from the cook's grunt and lack of another knee in her back, it was the right choice.

The stranger smiled at her. Unlike Mister Jankyn's smirk, the fancy man's smile seemed real.

"I'm Reynard," he said. "Ahnchahntay."

Patience figured that was probably fancy townfolk talk for 'pleased to meet you,' so she said that plain in return. With sirs on both ends, even.

Reynard held out his hand. He wore smooth, soft, black leather gloves. Patience hesitated. With his other hand, the fancy man patted the seat of the carriage. Miss Alys pushed her thumbs into Patience's shoulder blades.

"Go on then," she said without moving her mouth.

It was all most unusual. But the cook and the innkeeper waited, as if it was the thing for her to do. So, ignoring the stranger's helpful hand, Patience climbed into the carriage. With a little chuckle, Reynard climbed up after her.

"Not to worry," he said to Mister Jankyn — though it sounded to Patience like he was saying it for her benefit. "We'll have her back by the Witching Hour."

"Take all the time you need! You can always send us one of the Manor-girls to do her job."

Mister Jankyn laughed much too hard at his own joke. If it even was a joke. Patience couldn't tell. Either way, she didn't care for being traded away like a pig at the fair. Miss Alys still had her 'argue-and-get-whipped' face on though, so she held her peace.

"Thank you," Reynard said, turning his face to the road. "That will be all."

He stroked his ginger whiskers once on each side. He took up the reins. He clucked the horse. The carriage rattled off over the cobbles.

Patience sat back for the ride. She wasn't at all sure what was going on, but if this was how they did things in Whosebourne, this was how they did things. She supposed she should too.

*Who's going to keep the gravy from lumping, I want to know.*

She didn't ask out loud. Miss Alys had been quite firm about not talking. So, as they rode along, Patience had to content her curiosity with little sidelong glances at Reynard. She wanted to suss him out. Up close and alone, there was something about him that didn't add up.

Like his coat. She'd thought it was fancy enough in the alley, but wedged in next to him, she could see the vivid red fabric was just plain dyed wool. And it was worn nearly through at the elbows, and missing a button on the left sleeve. The velvet black jodhpurs were, she would admit, holiday-nice, but they were far from clean. In fact, they were quite covered in animal hair. It was as if he spent his time rolling around with country hounds.

She was so absorbed in the puzzle of how he could present himself so proper and so shabby at the same time that she didn't notice he'd asked her a question.

"Huh? Whuh?" she found herself grunting. When she realized what she'd done, she blushed to the roots of her hair. He must think she was a total clod!

"I was merely wondering," he repeated with a wink, pretending to ignore her shame, "what you think of our little town?"

"Sir, I haven't seen much of it, sir."

He chuckled. "Oh, don't bother with that Servant Sandwich nonsense. I'm nobody more or less important than you."

His manner said he meant it. But he drove a carriage and, shabby or not, his clothes were finer than any Patience had ever seen. More contradictions.

"It's a dull old burgh," he continued, "with everything in its place. Every person too. Never anything new."

Patience thought of the offaltosser. "Foxbonnet! Nothing new? Sure but that can't be true."

She watched the town slip by. The streets were a-bustle with people in all kinds of clothes, with all kinds of faces, doing all kinds of things.

"Same and same and same again," Reynard insisted.

Patience didn't know whether to nod or shake her head. Sometimes people back home talked down their own things — whether their house-keeping or their children or their gardens — but they didn't really mean it. And they got quite cross if you agreed.

But Reynard seemed sincere. He watched all the different people milling about with a dim and downward eye.

"Dull as dishwater, every one."

"I think maybe it's quite nice."

Reynard chuckled in a pleasant, restrained way. "You're still quite new. And who knows what excitement you bring with you?"

Patience didn't have time to ask what he meant by that. The carriage pulled up to a sight that swept all questions away.

A vast estate loomed before them. A deep green lawn and perfect square gardens spread for acres and acres. At the center rose an enormous stone mansion. The building's dozens of windows blazed in the red fire of dusk. An iron fence ringed the grounds. It crawled with metal curlicues and vines. A key was wrought at the top of every thick bar. Men and women in uniforms like Reynard's strode briskly in and out and up and down.

The fly coach pulled through a great iron gate and stopped at the base of a large sweep of granite stairs that led up to an enormous pair of brass-knobbed doors.

"Fox in a bonnet!" Patience exclaimed. "You could fit four farms under that roof! Who needs all that house?"

"Pennywhack Manor is home to none other than the Keyreeve," Reynard said. "Leader of the whole of Whosebourne. And my boss," he added as an afterthought.

"Flying fox in a solid gold hat," Patience whispered. "And what's he want with me?"

"That," Reynard swept down from the coach, "you'll just have to come inside and see."

## 4. Coinquaff and Shivtickle

Reynard knelt down and offered a knee to Patience as a step down from the carriage. She hopped to the cobbles without his help.

"Thank you." She curtsied to let him know she appreciated the offer, even if she didn't need it.

Reynard bowed most elegantly. At the bottom of the bow, a smirk flickered across his face. It was gone by the time he stood up. Patience had no idea what that was about.

"Let's see what this Keyreeve wants."

She marched up the granite steps toward the gleaming oak doors.

"No, no!" Reynard called after. He pointed round the side of the stairway. "People like us aren't go-in-the-front folk."

He led her to a small blue door with peeling paint, tucked away nearly unseen under the stairs. It hardly seemed right to Patience to invite someone to your house, then make them sneak in the side. The town, she reminded herself once again, was not the country.

She followed Reynard through the door and up two flights of narrow stairs that smelled of sweat, dust, and stale pipe-smoke. He wound her round and round a maze of small offices, bare-board hallways, and even closets. She could not have found her way back to the street on her own.

At length they came to a small room crammed with three desks, four chairs, and a sullen smudge of a fire. A plain wooden screen hid one corner. The edge of a cot poked out from behind it. The room smelled rather lived-in (like an animal's den), but Patience politely refrained from comment.

"Home sweet home." Reynard rolled his eyes as if he did not think much of it.

He took off his coat and tossed it onto the screen. He squeezed in behind one of the desks. He motioned for Patience to take the chair by the fire, which she did.

"Now," he put his boots on the desk and clasped his hands behind his head, "we wait for our betters."

Patience had no doubt. Reynard did not mean 'betters'. Quite the opposite. She was beginning to suspect that the ginger-whiskered man was mostly sarcastic and did not take his place in the world seriously.

She couldn't make up her mind whether that was a good or a bad thing.

Somewhere very close by, the Town Bell rang six times. At the dying of the sixth toll, a loud HNNGH! burst from behind the wooden screen.

"Gruffle!" Patience had meant to say 'gracious' but was too startled to get the word right.

Two enormous feet in soiled wool socks hit the floor at the end of the cot with a WHUPF! that shook her chair. A hulking man rose from the cot—and kept rising. He stood and stood, till he loomed over the screen, twice Patience's height. His shoulders stooped so he'd fit under the ceiling.

He made the room smaller just be being in it.

"Ah. Is it time for the night shift already?" Reynard said. "Miss Fell, I present my associate, Shivtickle."

BRAAAAP! An odious belch sounded from behind the gargantuan Shivtickle.

"And his associate," Reynard gave the tiniest roll of his eyes, "Coinquaff."

A short man without a straight line on his body rolled around Shivtickle's side. He leered at Patience, smacking his dry lips.

Reynard finished the introductions. "Coinquaff, Shivtickle, this is Miss Patience Fell."

A deep rumble drifted down from the ceiling. "Is it now?"

"What do you know about that?" Coinquaff rasped in a thirsty fashion.

The two reminded Patience of the sort of men who made the common room at *The Crock and Dice* go quiet just by walking in. Men who lived in the country woods and robbed the highways for sport. Men, as her father would say, who'd make a wolf walk the long way round to steer clear.

*What are men like that doing in a fancy place like this?*

Whatever the reason, Reynard showed no concern. They were wearing the same kind of red coat with a key on the lapel as he was. Patience curtsied in her chair as best she could (with Shivtickle standing, there was no room to get up).

"Very nice to meet you," she said, without much conviction.

They glanced at Reynard, as if checking with him what to do. He gave a quick little nod. They bowed without a bit of grace.

"Nice to meet you," they mumbled, not quite in unison.

"These gentlemen are the night shift at Pennywhack Manor," Reynard said. "And so they were just leaving."

The way he said the second part, it sounded to Patience like an order.

"Yes, sir." Coinquaff staggered out. Shivtickle squeezed through the door after him — much to Patience's relief.

"My apologies," Reynard said when they were gone. "I know they're quite grotesque. But one doesn't always get to choose who shares one's place in the world, does one?"

"I suppose not." But she thought, *I'd find a different place, if that was who I had to share it with.*

A tiny silver bell hanging over the door tinkled once, with a short and masterly sound.

"That'll be us." Reynard shrugged his coat back on.

Still unsettled by the two brutish men, Patience followed him back out into the servants' halls.

# 5. The Keyreeve

Patience found herself in a large office with a great bay window that overlooked the front of Pennywhack Manor. A desk the size of a barn door dominated the middle of the room. Its polished mahogany top gleamed in the lamplight. The man behind it gleamed too, though not (Patience assumed) from being polished. He was the pinkest man she'd ever seen.

Gold buttons shaped like keys strained to contain a shimmering red silk coat round his white-rufflepuffed chest. A tiny white wig perched atop the dome of his many-jowled head, like a sparrow nest balanced on the peak of a cottage roof. The wig wobbled as the man frowned down his nose at a single sheet of paper. He held it pinched in his sausage fingers, like a scrap of something unpleasant from the trash heap.

Patience stifled a giggle. Anyone that serious begged to be laughed at. If that was Reynard's boss, she understood why he was so sarcastic all the time.

"This is the one you told me about?" he gestured with the page.

"Sir, yes Keyreeve, sir," Reynard replied.

"Fetch my nephew."

Reynard bowed. He vanished, closing the door behind him. Patience noticed that, from this side the door had been cleverly built; disguised as part of the wall. How many other doors might be hidden along the Manor's walls, to keep the servants out of sight?

Alone with the Keyreeve, Patience wasn't sure what came next. He ignored her. For want of a better idea, she tried a curtsy. She was quite good at it, if she did say so herself.

The Keyreeve continued to frown at the paper in front of him. It couldn't possibly have taken him that long to read it.

If that's how he was going to be, she might as well take the place in. She'd never been anywhere near as fancy.

The desk, for instance, had been buffed so shiny, it reflected the whole room, all tiny and stretched out. It was empty, except for one large leather-bound book. Patience turned her head sideways to read the title.

*THE CHAOS COURT*

*Hrm. Same book as Miss Crowquill. I bet his copy isn't all covered in leek juice though.*

The Keyreeve rumbled and leaned back in his chair. He continued to act like she wasn't there. Someone else might have felt awkward or small in the enormous silence of the room, but Patience was used to being ignored. If he wanted to invite her in and then pretend like she was part of the furniture, that was his business. She went back to inspecting the room.

Portraits of men and women in fancy clothes, striking fancy poses, covered the walls. Statues of people from the chest up sneered down their noses at her from alcoves. The whole ceiling was painted like sky and clouds, with naked babies with wings unrolling the corners like a blanket.

*I'd be nervous if babies without diapers were flying over my head all day.* She'd changed her brothers and sisters often enough to imagine what a bad thing *that* would be.

What drew her attention most, though, was the least fancy thing in the room. In a glass-topped display case on a snow white cushion rested a small iron key, as common as could be.

*Why on Earth is that here?*

"The Key to the Town," the Keyreeve said.

Caught up in the chaos of the room's décor, Patience hadn't noticed he'd been watching her.

"'Tis but a symbol of my authority," he continued, "as the leader of this fine community."

"It's very nice," she said, forgetting the 'sirs' on either end.

The Keyreeve snorted. Patience knew it was impossible to speak while snorting, but she was positive he had somehow said the word 'bumpkin.' She'd never heard the word, but she could guess what it meant. She didn't care for it. Not one bit.

Before she could take the Keyreeve to task for rudeness, the door to the office opened — the regular door that looked like a door, not the servant door Patience had come in.

She expected to see Reynard. Instead, a boy her own age bustled breathlessly in. He wore a miniature version of the Keyreeve's outfit, though the vest-buttons were off by one and the shirt was half-untucked. His wig was askew.

"Present, Uncle," he wheezed, taking a place next to the enormous desk. He squinted at Patience through thick, smudged glasses.

"Brubarubaruba!" the Keyreeve rumbled. "Enough pleasantries. I'm a busy man. Brubaruba. To the point. It has been made known to me that you claim to have seen a—," he consulted the page he was holding, "—cursing whirlwind of trash in the alley of one *Crock and Dice*, a tavern and boarding establishment in the Fairgate neighborhood."

That caught her off guard. In two hundred years she never would've guessed the Keyreeve would summon her over an offaltosser.

"S-sir, I—"

"BOSH!"

BANG! The Keyreeve slammed his hand on *The Chaos Court*. His wig jumped. Patience and the boy squeaked in unison.

"Stuff and nonsense!" the Keyereeve rumbled.

With some effort, he leaned over the desk. The rolls of his brow nearly swallowed up his eyes.

"Simple servant superstition. We Whosebournians have no need of this kind of huckstery. Stirs up the populace. Creates kerfluffle. Bad. For. Business."

He punctuated the last three words with three sausage-jabs on the book's cover.

Patience wanted to say something to defend herself. She hadn't asked for a filthy trash man to yell curses at her on her first day in town. And she certainly hadn't told anyone afterward. But she knew all about being yelled at by grown-ups; there was no point in talking back. Best wait till he was done, then be on her way.

"Whatever it is you *think* you saw can doubtless be explained easily enough without resorting to childish country fantasies. Therefore," he concluded in a softer tone, "if anyone asks you about it, you are to say 'I saw nothing unusual at all.'"

The boy blinked, startled. He frowned. "Uncle, is that—"

"Brubarubaruba!" The Keyreeve turned himself in his nephew's general direction. He fixed him with a gimlet eye.

The boy lowered his head. "Sorry, sir," he mumbled. But the frown never left his face.

The Keyreeve leaned back in his chair. It groaned like a cow about to calve. If the chair collapsed, Patience wondered, would he fall to the floor or would he keep going right on through to the room below? She could see it going either way.

"Well?" he interrupted her speculation. "Can you say that?"

In her mind, she reviewed what he'd said. "I saw nothing unusual at all?"

"Good! But try it again, without the vacillation. Put some belief into it, girl!"

"I saw nothing unusual at all." It didn't sound right at all. Judging from the way the Keyreeve's nephew frowned even harder at the floor, he heard it the same way.

The Keyreeve smiled. He might have been trying to be jolly, but he reminded her of a cow with a stomach full of air.

"Good girl. Now you practice that all the way home. And if anyone asks you about offaltossers or other such Chaos Court nonsense, you will tell them..."

"I saw nothing unusual at all."

The lie did not improve with repetition. But it satisfied the Keyreeve. He smiled his gassy-cow smile. He stomped a button on the floor. A tiny silver bell tinkled behind her. Reynard slipped into the room through the servant's door, his footfalls soft as a fox in the forest. The Keyreeve hoisted his bulk to the window with a HARRUMPH.

"You may take her away."

Reynard led her back outside to the coach.

## 6. The Cobblemauler

Her meeting with the Keyreeve left Patience cross. Of all the inexplicable, stupid-seeming things grown-ups had asked her to do in twelve years on Earth, lying had never been one of them. Till now. It did not sit well.

As they rode along, Reynard kept up a breezy stream of chatter; tidbits about the passing buildings and monuments. He had a fact for every sight and a sarcastic aside to go with it. He was quite knowledgeable, especially about Whosebourne's history. But Patience didn't pay attention to any of it. She was lost in grumpy thought.

*Who's this Keyreeve anyway? Who made him Lord High Give-Orders? Maybe I'll just tell everyone about the offaltosser. Maybe I'll shout it from the highest rooftop. See what he does then.*

That was the problem. Who knew what he might do? The worst punishment she'd ever gotten back home was a whipping with a switch. She could take that. She could take that all day long, if it meant being honest. But maybe they had worse in Whosebourne.

Probably they had worse.

*Maybe I'll just... maybe I could... maybe, maybe, maybe I don't know what I'm doing and there's no one to tell me.*

Glaring at nothing with savage fury, she thought a few of the words the offaltosser had said.

The carriage stopped.

Patience expected to find herself back at *The Crock and Dice*. Instead, they were in a large open space, surrounded by boarded-up buildings.

"Fairgate Square," Reynard intoned. No flippant comment followed.

Patience peered across the dim plaza. At the center, where she'd expect a statue or fountain, there stood only a plain iron gate. It was no higher than a tall man's head. It stood by itself, not even raised on a platform or graced by a plaque. A large padlock held it shut; entirely unnecessary, as it led nowhere. There was neither fence nor wall around it. Only a gate in an empty square, rusting away to no end.

"Why bother?"

Reynard answered in a low and serious tone. "None of the plain folk remember why the Fairgate is there. Who knows where..." he trailed off.

As plain as the gate was, Patience couldn't help but stare. She had the distinct impression that she should be able to see something through it—something *other* than the other side of the square.

"Who knows where it goes?" she echoed Reynard and finished his sentence.

Reynard shook off his somberness with a laugh. "To the other side of the square, of course. Between you and me, it's as silly as can be. But what can you do? Public works. Pfft." He sniffed dismissively. "On we go."

He clucked the horse into motion.

Patience was not so easily distracted. She craned her neck to keep an eye on the gate. Something important was going on there. No matter what Reynard said.

"Can we just—"

THUNK! KAKRACK!

The coach lurched hard to one side. Patience cried out and went flying. With one strong arm, Reynard caught her. The coach's clatter took on a limping lilt. It rocked badly side-to-side down the street.

"Whoa!" Reynard called out to the horse. She trotted to a slow stop.

"Are you hurt?" he asked Patience.

Her heart raced. She patted herself up and down. She shook her head.

"Good, good." He jumped down from the carriage. "I don't know where I'd find another broom-girl this late in the day."

Patience cackled, more loudly than the joke deserved. The near-crash had left her spooked as a sheep who'd seen the shears. Her hands were shaking. She took a deep breath. She closed her eyes and took another. She pushed her hands on the carriage seat to stop the tremble. She opened her eyes. The red-yellow burst of excitement receded into the black night.

"What happened?" She joined Reynard beside the coach.

"There," he pointed at the front wheel. "A fine bother."

Even in the dim light, Patience could see clear. The wheel was broken. It had twisted in a perfectly round hole in the street, where a cobblestone had been neatly plucked out. She noticed several other places along the road that were also missing cobbles.

"Lucky we always keep a spare under the frame."

Patience held the horse's head and stroked her nose while Reynard took off his red coat and laid it on the carriage seat. He retrieved the spare. He propped it up on the side of the fly so he could change it out.

It was a lengthy process that involved a great deal of grease and grunting. Patience would have offered to help, but Reynard growled as he worked—like her father changing a wagon wheel. And she imagined that, like her father, he would snap at her if she interrupted him.

As she waited, her attention wandered. The night-time town was no noisier than the country, but the kinds of noises were all new to her. She heard hoarse coughs and bursts of sudden laughter, splashes of water dumped from high windows and annoyed shouts right after. Doors slammed and windows rattled. An over-fierce dog barked at nothing till its owner shouted 'quiet!' A muffled voice sang a tune with slurred words into the uncaring night.

Gradually Patience became aware of a sound under all that ruckus; a persistent but inconsistent tapping. It came from an alley nearby. At first, there were many short, quick raps. Then came several precise taps, separated by long intervals. After that, the short, quick raps started again.

*What is that? Whosebourne doesn't have midnight woodpeckers, do they? No. That makes no sense.*

Reynard had reached a forceful point in the wheel-changing process. He would be at it for a while. Rather than stand around useless, Patience went to investigate the unusual noise. She crept to where the alley met the street. She widened her eyes as big as they would go, to see what little the dim might show.

At the far end of the alley she spied a wee man—the same size as the offaltosser!

Her fingers curled. But her broom hung on its hook, all the way back at *The Crock and Dice*. Unarmed, she took one cautious step into the darkness.

It was not an offaltosser.

Unlike the trash-throwing little fellow, this man was quite clean — if a bit stubbly. Small as he was, he appeared very muscular. He wore an orange vest that caught the street lamp's glow and a tiny yellow helmet. He stood in a puddle of lamplight between two piles of cobblestones, one considerably larger than the other.

*Careful now,* Patience thought to herself, *if he starts throwing those, you're a goner.*

She crouched low. She kept to the shadows. She slid along the wall, close as she dared.

One-handed, the wee man hoisted a cobble from the smaller pile. With ease! Patience couldn't believe it, given his size and the size of the stone. It was as if she had hoisted an entire hay-wagon all by herself.

She ducked even lower. This was not someone to trifle with.

But the wee man didn't throw the rock.

Instead, he turned it this way and that, inspecting it in the lamplight. He snuffled it. He tasted it with a quick dab of his tongue. He lifted a miniature pick hammer in his free hand. He tapped the stone several times quickly. Nothing happened. He tossed it on the large heap and selected another cobble from the dwindling pile.

*There you go,* Patience told herself, *now you know what that sound was. Back away quietly and go home.*

She did not move. This was too interesting. If there had been any more shadows between her and the little man, she would have gotten even closer.

He tapped a new rock. Immediately, a faint answer-tap came from within.

Patience clapped her hand over her mouth to keep from gasping aloud.

The wee man danced a merry caper. His vest flashed and his helmet almost fell off his head. He swung the tapping cobble about with joy.

Composing himself, he set it carefully down. It wobbled back and forth. It reminded Patience of an egg about to hatch.

The tiny strongman leaned his pick against it. He spat on his hands and rubbed them together. He picked up the hammer with both fists. With a blow so mighty it lifted him from his feet, he hit the wobbling cobble.

It split in two. Another wee man, identical in every way to the first (down to the helmet and vest) stood in the rubble. The two fellows shook hands firmly.

Patience couldn't contain herself anymore.

"FOXBONNET!"

She toppled out of the shadows in surprise.

Both men jumped and spun round mid-air. She and they stared at each other for a moment. The wee men in bright orange vests scuttled away into the dark, disappearing down a storm grate.

"All done!" Reynard called from the street.

Keeping one eye on the alleyway, Patience returned to the fly. She opened her mouth, shut it, opened it again, then shut it one more time.

"Are you quite well?" Reynard asked, helping her into the carriage.

"I-I saw nothing unusual at all," she said. Exactly like she'd been told.

The lie sounded more ridiculous every time she said it.

## 7. Back to the Attic

When she got back to *The Crock and Dice*, Patience was relieved to find Miss Alys asleep. The cook would probably have all kind of questions. Patience didn't want to lie to her, but telling the truth wouldn't go well either.

She could just picture it.

*"Oh yes, Miss Alys, the Keyreeve what runs the whole town called me into his office to tell me he knew I'd seen an offaltosser. What's that? Offaltosser? Why just a magical invisible little man what throws trash around until you hit him with a broom. Crazy Miss Crowquill's got a book explains it all. Just ask her. As I was saying, the fanciest man in Fancyland told me not to tell anyone about seeing this offaltosser and sent me off. Why am I so late getting back? 'Cause on the way home the carriage crashed in a hole made by a little man who breaks rocks to find even more little men…"*

At that point, she imagined Miss Alys would whack *her* with a broom until she ran off.

Maybe that was what had happened to the last girl who left *The Crock and Dice* in tears.

*Best not to wonder.* She had a long day's work waiting in the morning. She crawled into bed. She pulled the covers over her head and ordered herself to go to sleep.

It didn't work.

She tried thrashing. She tried laying perfectly still. She counted sheep. She counted goats. She counted cows and chickens and every other barnyard animal she knew. None of it worked.

Every time she closed her eyes, she saw a host of wee people. Behind them all, the Keyreeve loomed, shaking his sausage-finger at her and saying: "You see nothing unusual at all."

Something occurred to her. It had been staring her in the face, but with all that had happened, she hadn't thought of it till then. She sat up.

*How did the Keyreeve know I'd seen the offaltosser?*

It was a good question. She hadn't told anyone. Miss Alys had come outside after he'd run off. And there hadn't been anyone else in the alley.

Anyone that she could see, at any rate.

There was only one other person who knew all about the offaltosser incident. Only one person could have told the Keyreeve.

*Miss Crowquill.*

As carefully as she could, so as not to wake Miss Alys, Patience snuck out of the servants' bedroom. The door creaked when she opened it. The exhausted cook snuffled.

"Oats…" she mumbled before settling back into a steady snore.

One slow step at a time, Patience crept up the stairs. The sleeping inn made many noises, none louder than the *thump-thump* of her heart.

She remembered all the stories they told back home about the stocks in the Whosebourne public square. If you broke the rules, the people in charge would lock you up, hands and ankles. Everyone in town would throw rotten cabbages at you while you baked all day in the sun.

*You'll end up smelling like an offaltosser.*

That might be. But she wanted answers. She shoved the fear away and slipped up through the night.

The attic ladder was already down. Light from above cast a pale square on the floor under the open trapdoor. She wasn't sure whether being expected made her feel less worried, or more.

She decided it didn't matter.

"In for an offal, in for a toss," she muttered and climbed the ladder.

Miss Crowquill was even more disheveled than the morning Patience had met her. She sat on her unmade bed, holding a crumpled page in each fist. The pages were smeared. To her surprise, Patience saw streaks of ink under the woman's eyes.

Her determination to get answers vanished.

"Is everything alright, ma'am? I'm sure everything will be alright." She tried to curtsy in a consoling fashion.

Crowquill ruffled puffs of grey down from her hair. She blew out an UGH!

"I haven't had a friend at my window in five mornings and it puts me quite out of sorts. When the blackbird leaves me by, I will fuss and cuss and cry…"

Being reminded of the rumpled woman's strange interchange with the crow set Patience back on task. It was time to be practical. She took a firm stand and stuck out her chin.

"Are you a witch?"

Crowquill's black eyes glittered in the low lamp light. "Would it matter?"

*Would it?*

Back in the country, witches were still kindled from time to time. Patience wanted no truck with witches.

On the other hand, the kinds of things she'd been seeing could probably only be explained by a witch — or something as bad as a witch, anyway. And she did want explanations. Slowly, she shook her head.

"Of course it wouldn't. But lucky for your peace of mind, I am not a witch."

Patience furrowed her brow.

"It's true!" Crowquill shook a feather out of her hair. "I'm not!"

One eyebrow arched up from Patience's frown. "You're awful knowy for someone who stays in the attic all day and night."

Crowquill rose from the bed. She paced to the casement that overlooked the alley. The moonlight washed her face clean of color. In a low voice, so Patience had to lean in to hear her, she recited a little verse.

"Lady Crowquill, with a curious eye
watches the world pass her by.
She whistles a tune and blots a page
and struts and frets alone in her cage."

She stared far away out the window, very sad. She looked how Patience felt when she thought about home.

She turned back to Patience, all business—as all business as an ink-smudged woman with feather-filled ever-mussed hair could be, at any rate.

"But you're not here to learn about me. You crept up here pit-a-pat on slippered feet because strange things are a-doing down in the street."

"Yes! The street!"

Patience quickly told the story of the tiny men in vests, tearing up the streets to find more of their kind.

"Tu-whoo, whoo-tu, what a thing to do, to do!"

Crowquill danced across the room to a shelf. She plucked out a book. Patience recognized it as the same leek-stained volume with the entry on the offaltosser. *The Chaos Court* by Johnny Factotum. The same book the Keyreeve had on his desk.

"Chirrup-chirreep, chirreep-chirroo!" Crowquill leafed through her tome. She poked a page. "Aha! Here! Johnny always knows."

Patience took the heavy book. She read, puzzling it out loud as she went.

### The Cobblemauler

*This common Rhyme about the Cobblemauler is chanted by Oldwives and Greybeards alike:*

*Awake at Night in a City or Town*
*You might hear the Tap of a wee Hammer sound*
*'Tis the Cobblemauler, Cobblemauler, making his Rounds.*

*These small Folk inhabit Towns of middling to great Size and do damage the Streets with their persistent Excavations, much to the Chagrin and Annoy of Officials and Coachmen alike. Common Wits disagree on whether They remove the Cobbles in search of Treasure or out of Malice towards Carriages, but Doctors agree that such little Men do hatch, fully grown in orange Vests, from Eggs that do resemble themselves Cobblestones. For this Reason, it is the Opinion of the Wise that these Cobble-eggs were oft us'd in the laying of Streets and that the Cobblemaulers do merely seek their Kin and Offspring for to nurse Them and bring forth more of their Kind into the World.*

That was all. The next entry was titled 'The Coinquaff' but Patience didn't see the point in reading it. However highly Crowquill thought of this Johnny Factotum fellow, his book wasn't very useful.

"So they're looking for their eggs? Is that all?" She couldn't blame them for that.

"You're not scared?"

"Why? They're just chickens with picks and vests instead of pecks and feathers."

Crowquill tittered. "I never thought of it that way!"

Patience stared at her like a dog stares at sheep. "You know all about all of this."

"Yes."

"You've got this book that tells about offaltossers and cobblemaulers."

"And appletopplers and quibblemuches and the whole rest of the Chaos Court! My Johnny is ever so clever!"

"Then why — WHY — haven't you done anything about it?!" Patience snapped the book shut with a WHUFF!

"AH!" Crowquill leapt into her bed. She pulled up her covers nearly to her head.

Patience let her stare repeat the question. It hung in the air till it was more awkward for Crowquill to say nothing than answer her.

"W-what could I do? I don't even have a broom."

That was so stupid, Patience couldn't reply. All the ways she could say it was wrong charged towards her mouth at once and got stuck in her throat. All that came out was an angry gurgle.

Crowquill didn't notice. She kept whimpering. "Besides, there's more than just the little ones. There's," her voice dropped to a whisper, "the Marquis."

Before Patience could ask, the town bell sounded five times.

"Almost day, almost day!" Crowquill hid 'neath the covers. "Time for you to go away."

Outside the window, Patience saw the blue light of just-before-dawn.

"Dreck and drettel!"

She was all the way downstairs before she realized she was still holding Crowquill's book. By then, it was too late to do anything but hide the bulky tome under her pillow. Miss Alys stirred in bed. Breakfast needed making.

# 8. Linus Pennywhack

All day long, Patience's mind was not on her work. She slopped lunch stew into the fire while stirring. She drifted off while scrubbing the trenchers, leaving a crust of meaty grease on them. She put knives in the fork drawer, forks in the spoon drawer, and spoons into a big sack of potatoes.

When she poured salt into the sugar bowl, Miss Alys had enough.

"One ride in a fancy carriage to the Keyreeve's house and she thinks she's too good to be a broom-girl!"

"Ma'am, sorry, ma'am." Patience curtsied. Her face got hot. "I don't think that, I promise."

"Oh no? I know how it is with you girls from the country who come to the town. Don't get your head all turned round trying to climb to a high place in the world." The cook waggled one crooked finger at her. "You'll slip and I'll wave as you pass by, tumbling all the way back down.

"Ma'am, yes, ma'am," Patience said, curt and cross — not at Miss Alys, but at herself. She did not like doing a bad job.

The cook went on and on for quite some time. She lectured Patience through the whole of supper-making and on until well after the last of the dishes were cleaned and put away for the day.

All the while, Patience kept her head down, hiding the shame in her face as she worked to undo her mistakes. She was mortified that Miss Alys thought so little of her, but she couldn't argue. It was all her fault. She'd let weird little men and bellowing Keyreeves and a mad attic woman get in the way of doing her proper job in her proper place. No two ways about it.

The worst of it was she couldn't even explain to Miss Alys (who asked several times) *why* she'd messed up, explain that it wasn't because she thought herself 'high and mighty and above her place.'

What could she say? If the cook was angry about some salted sugar, Patience could only imagine her reaction to tales of tiny men and old leeky books and sneaking about the attic in the midnight hour.

So she shoved all thoughts of cobblemaulers and Crowquill and Chaos Courts out of her head. She promised herself she'd take that useless book back to the attic and forget the whole mess. In the mean time, she worked harder than ever before, sweeping with a savage fury till the fire dwindled and it was time for bed.

"Alright girl," Miss Alys said, in a more kindly tone. She took the broom from Patience's blistered hands. "That's enough for today. Set your mind to do better tomorrow and you'll never know a night of sorrow."

That was something Patience's mother used to say. It meant that everything between them was okay.

The next day was normal as could be. And the next. By the third day, Patience had almost convinced herself she'd put a stop to all the fox-bonnet oddness, by will and hard work alone. The only piece of unfinished business was returning Crowquill's book and that was just a matter of finding a moment to spare.

Then the boy showed up.

She noticed him before she really noticed him. When Miss Alys bustled through the kitchen door to the common room, Patience caught a glimpse of him, sitting close to the front of the inn and looking quite out of place. She stopped scouring the loaf pan. The kitchen door swung shut.

*What was I doing?*

She shook her head. She couldn't remember why she'd stopped, so she went back to scrubbing.

When Miss Alys came back in, the boy had moved up, one chair closer to the kitchen. That got her attention. Out of the corner of her eye, she tried to see as much of him as she could see before the door closed again.

There was something familiar about him. He was about her age. But he wasn't one of the boys from back home.

"Ale! Trice lunch!" Miss Alys barked. She jabbed with tongs at three giant sausages, sizzling in a skillet.

Patience filled up three mugs and set them on a tray. She spun round to the plate cupboard, took out three plates, set them on the counter nearest the stove, and added a generous helping of boiled cabbage and onions to each one. She ducked under Miss Alys as the cook tossed the sausages one at a time onto the plates. She took each plate as the sausage hit it and transferred it to the tray.

She and Miss Alys had gotten the dance of preparation down pat.

When Patience went back to the dishes, she positioned herself so she could keep an eye on the door.

Sure enough, the boy had moved one chair closer to the kitchen again. He wore clothes that she supposed were trying to be plain, but couldn't hide their fancy. He squinted round the room through thick-smudged glasses.

*I know you…*

She couldn't for the life of her remember how.

Miss Alys came and went several more times. Each time, the boy had sidled closer to the kitchen. Patience caught him eyeing her intently. He glanced away, pretending (badly) that he'd just been idly gazing round.

Finally, he sat right beside the door. The cook swept by him. He charged into the kitchen behind her back.

"Patience Fell?" The way he asked sounded as if he already knew the answer, but wanted to be double extra sure.

Patience gripped the skillet she was scouring. She didn't think the boy was up to mischief, but best not take the chance. She nodded.

He lurched towards her. She stood up and backed away.

"P-pennywhack M-manor," the boy stammered. "M-midnight. Give the gate-guard this."

Before she could react, he lunged past her. He smelled like soap and roses. He shoved a wad of paper into her hand as he passed. He scurried right out the back door into the alley.

That's when she remembered where she'd seen him. He'd been wearing a crooked wig and standing behind the Keyreeve's desk.

She uncrumpled the page.

*To whomever is on guard duty,*

*Please admit the bearer of this note. She is expected. Show her to the Widow's Walk.*

*-Linus Pennywhack*

There was a detailed drawing of a key under the signature.

"Fox in a bonnet," she grumbled. "I'm not going. I'm not."

She stuffed the note into her apron and went back to work.

## 9. The Widow's Walk

She wasn't going to go. She told herself it was none of her business as she climbed into bed. And she repeated that for two hours straight, staring at the ceiling wide awake.

Not. Her. Place.

It was remembering the look on the boy's face that changed her mind; his troubled expression when the Keyreeve told her to lie. It meant something very wrong was going on, no matter what most folk in Whosebourne might pretend. And at least one other person knew it—two if she counted mad Miss Crowquill in the attic.

"If one person thinks you're a donkey," she thought, "pay them no mind. If two people do, check how many carrots you eat."

She slipped out of bed and pit-patted through the kitchen to the street.

"And if three people think you're a donkey," she finished her mother's saying, "get yourself fitted for a saddle."

She found Pennywhack Manor again with surprising ease, even in the dark. Whosebourne was as big as a town could be, but there were lots of lamp-lit signs to all the important places. The last toll of the twelfth bell faded right as she reached the manor gate.

The moon had set. No lamps were lit on the grounds. The vast house loomed black, blotting out a wide swath of stars. Here and there a tiny sliver of light broke through a curtain crack. No one moved in the shadows.

The boy had told her to show his note to a gate-guard.

"Hello?" she whispered to the night on the other side of the iron fence.

"Brrraaaappp!" A noxious fume wafted through the bars.

*Hssshh-pop.*

A match flared, revealing a small guard hut right by the gate. Wedged in it was a round man with bleary eyes and a wobbly head. Patience recognized him from Reynard's little room.

He shoved the flame into a brass lantern. When the wick lit, he spit on the tip of the match and flicked it into a thicket. He lifted the lamp and squinted.

"Mister Coinquaff?" She remembered Reynard had called the belchy man 'the night shift'.

"Whozzat?" He smacked his lips. "Oh. S'you. Practical Plummet."

"Patience Fell." Why was this so difficult? She remembered people's names just fine.

"Suit yourself." He settled back into the hut. His heavy-lidded eyes fluttered shut. A low drone sputtered out of his lips.

"Oi!"

She said it more loudly than she intended. Coinquaff jumped, bumping his head. The sound echoed across the lawn in front of the mansion. She half-expected all the lights to come on, the front door to fling open, and an angry Keyreeve to bumble brubarubarubaing out.

Instead, the echo of her *Oi!* faded away. The house and grounds remained night-silent.

After a moment of quiet, a low cruel chuckle seeped down from high above her head. A patch of darkness, blotting out almost as many of the stars as the house itself, moved towards the gate. The enormous Mister Shivtickle stepped into the smudge cast by Coinquaff's lamp. His eyes glittered yellow and black.

"This one's got spirit."

His voice made Patience want to run. But she had the boy's note and business to attend to. She fished it out of her pocket. She pushed it through the bars. It took all her effort, but she was proud her hand didn't tremble a bit.

"I'm expected." Her voice wasn't as steady as she might have liked, but it would do.

The hulking thug pinched the note in his long, long fingers. He unfolded it. He held it up to the light and made a great show of reading it. He wadded it into his coat pocket. He nodded to Coinquaff.

His associate squirmed around in the guard hut until he could reach behind himself. He extricated a wooden pole with a curve on the end—like a shepherd's crook. Without standing up, he extended the crook to the gate latch. He flipped up the latch, turned the hook, and tugged open the iron-barred gate just wide enough for Patience to slip through. After she entered, he reversed the process, ending by stowing the hook-pole who-knows-where and settling back with a heavy sigh.

Shivtickle picked up the lamp. Holding it at chin level, he leered down at her. His feet were in darkness. He jerked his head for her to follow.

"The Widow's Walk's this way."

She had been hoping Coinquaff would be the one to show her the way. Gassy, curt, and always-a-little-tipsy didn't worry her. But he was already back to snoring. And she wasn't going to wander around in the dark with the likes of Shivtickle. Townfolk might think his sort could be stuffed in a uniform and made to behave, but she'd believe it when she saw it a hundred times in a row—and maybe not then.

"Before sun-up," he rumbled from two steps down the path.

"Oh, there's no need," she called out, thinking furious fast. "You shouldn't leave your place."

She looked meaningfully at the burbling Coinquaff and rolled her eyes. "Best there be two on watch. You can just tell me where to go and I can find the way."

"Ain't that considerate of you." The brute sneered at her, as if to say *I know you're afraid of me, little girl.*

She didn't care if he told everyone in Whosebourne she was the biggest coward in twenty counties. She wasn't stupid as the rooster who danced into a fox's den just to prove he was brave.

"Directions, if you please." She even curtsied.

"Oh, you'll do nice," he said. It was an odd thing to say; likely it meant something nasty.

"Directions?" she repeated. "Master Linus is expecting me." The sooner she could get to the boy, the better she'd feel about things.

"Down to the blue door where you first came in." Shivtickle jerked a thumb towards the manor. "Don't go inside. Follow the hedge-path close along the wall. You'll see the way up to the Widow's Walk halfway down the house."

With that, he shuttered the lantern. Patience perked her ears. She could hear his great big boots crunching on the gravel. His shadow against the stars moved away until the night sky shone clear again.

*You might have left the lamp.*

But she wouldn't have him bring it back, not for all the daylight in summer. *Good riddance to brute thuggish,* she thought, putting her own twist on something her father liked to say after unpleasant people left the room.

Even without the lamp, her wide eyes had enough starlight to find the door and the path. She stepped careful around the sleeping manor. She kept one hand on the cold stone wall and one ear out for a heavy crunch of boots — just in case Shivtickle tried to sneak up on her.

About halfway down the house, her fingers brushed an iron rung, sunk into the wall. She strained upwards; three more were set, one above the other. Beyond that, she assumed the ladder went on clear up to the flat black line of the roof.

*What an odd place to send a guest.*

She almost went home right then. It had to be a prank. Boys back home were always playing pranks. The Keyreeve's nephew might be town-fancy, but a boy was a boy. She'd probably climb halfway up and find out he'd greased the rungs or they'd disappear into the house or something. All the lights would come on and everyone would have a good laugh at the country bumpkin stuck on the side of the mansion.

*On the other hand, if you wanted to keep the Keyreeve away...*

She couldn't picture the enormous bewigged man hoisting himself up the side of his house. It'd be like the cow going over the moon. And the boy had been secretive when he'd handed her the note. He could have chosen the meeting place to make sure his uncle stayed out of it.

Prank or clever way to keep a secret? Either one made equal sense. The choice was hers.

"In for a crow, in for a quill," she muttered and scampered up Pennywhack Manor to the Widow's Walk.

## 10. The Boy Who Showed Patience the Stars

It wasn't a prank.

The rungs led all the way up the side of the house and over the slant of the roof. Up top, the roof's peak gave way to railing. The wood rails enclosed a wide, flat expanse that ran a quarter the length of the building. On one end of the walk, a platform covered in a domed roof hung out over empty air. On the other end was a door that, Patience presumed, led into the manor.

*Thanks for showing me the hard way, Mister Shivtickle.* His kind had to be mean about even the little things.

She stepped over the railing. The boy, Linus, stood out on the platform with his back to her. He hadn't heard her arrive. She drew closer quietly, taking a moment to suss him out by the low light of his half-hooded lantern.

He was fiddling with a brass contraption. A long tube pointed up at the stars, atop a tripod. There were knobs on the side that he turned with delicate clicks. He bobbed up and down over a smaller tube sticking at a right angle out of the larger one. He consulted a small notebook and muttered to himself; words Patience had never heard, like 'azimuth' and 'declension.'

*Are you a wizard?*

He certainly wasn't like any boy she'd ever met. He was serious and fussy and clumsily mussed. But watching him work, she couldn't imagine him being anything so threatening as a wizard.

She cleared her throat.

"AH!" He jumped and spun round mid-air. His elbow hit the brass tube, knocking it cattywompus.

"Take care!" She reached out and steadyed him so he wouldn't tumble over the rails.

"M-much ob-bliged." He pushed his crooked glasses back straight. He squinted at her through smudged lenses. "P-p-patience F-fell?"

"You said to come at midnight?" She *thought* she remembered that's what he said. But he was so surprised to see her, she second-guessed herself.

"Gracious!" Wheezing, he fumbled at his waist-coat. He produced a silver pocket watch. Holding it up close to his face, he peered at the time. "It's already ten past!"

"Sorry about that," she said. "I did get here at twelfth bell. I hadn't planned on the climb."

"C-climb? W-what on earth are you talking about?" Before she could answer, he whirled round. "My telescope!"

Linus bent back over his contraption.

"Pardon my distraction," he said. "I want to ascertain the corrective measures for the recent jostling. If my calculations are correct — which they almost always are — it was pointed precisely at the planet before my indelicate startlement knocked the instrument out of alignment."

Patience worked on figuring out what he was saying while he worked on his telescope. She noticed that when he used big words and focused on his tools, his stutter and wheeze disappeared. As if the work settled him, the stutter did not return.

"There we go." He stood back up. He nodded, satisfied. "No harm done."

"That's good." She realized she hadn't once used the Servant Sandwich. He didn't seem to notice. "Sorry again about scaring you."

"No apologies necessary. If anything, it is I who should offer them to you. I get absorbed. Where are my manners? Linus Pennywhack, at your service."

He bowed. He smiled at her in such a friendly fashion, she couldn't help but smile back. They stood there smiling at one another and not saying a thing. It got awkward, but Patience hadn't a clue how to break the stalemate. Was he waiting for her to say something? He was the one who had asked her to visit.

At last, Linus clapped his hands.

"Right then," he said. "Right then, right then, right then. Right then." He blinked and shook his head. "The first thing is for me to stop saying 'right then.'"

She laughed and he joined her. With that, she felt it would be fine to come right out and ask.

"Why did you want to see me?"

"Ah. That." He clasped his hands behind his back. It reminded Patience of her old schoolmaster. "I'm not from Whosebourne you see, and I was hoping that, as a local, you might shed light on my uncle's most strange behavior."

"I'm not from here either."

"Fancy that! Another country person!"

"You're from the country?" His talk was proper as could be. He wore a waistcoat, even at midnight. She couldn't imagine him rough-housing with country boys.

"The Pennywhacks have estates both in Whosebourne and the country, yes. I resided at the latter until sent to my uncle's house to find my place in the world. But that's neither here nor there. Even if you're not Whosebournian, you may be helpful."

A deep and serious expression settled on his face. "Anomalies abound in this town."

"I don't know about any of that," Patience said, "but some fox-bonnet odd things are happening, sure as a goose fancies a gander."

Linus frowned. "I'm not sure what barnyard fowl have to do with anything."

"What?"

"Never mind." He jiggered his glasses about his nose. "Let's begin. My uncle said you'd seen something impossible — or at least highly improbable. But instead of asking you more about it, he ordered you to prevaricate."

"He told me to lie is what he did." Every time she thought about it, it made her more angry.

"That's what I said."

*Then why didn't you just say it?* she thought. But she didn't say anything. She might be on the verge of making a friend and didn't want to spoil it by being snippy.

"He then intimated that you might be witness to other strange events. 'Chaos Court nonsense' were, I believe, his exact words."

"Yes! The Chaos Court. Just like Miss Crowquill's book!"

"Just like the book on uncle's desk. Which is the second strangest thing. My uncle, whatever his good qualities, is not a reader. That is, in fact, the first time I've ever see him with a book. When I asked him if I might borrow it, however, he rumbled at me to stick to learning my place."

"Brubarubaruba," Patience mimed a good jowl-shake.

"Ha! You're refreshingly free."

That was good enough for her. If he didn't mind her making fun of his uncle and he already knew *something* was going on, she might as well trust him enough to come clean about everything she knew.

She told him about the offaltosser and the cobblemaulers and about Crowquill in the attic with her birds and words. She told him about what little she'd read of *The Chaos Court*, old and confusing as it was. She told him about the girl who'd fled *The Crock and Dice* on Patience's very first day in Whosebourne, leaving a place in the world for her.

He listened to it all with an intense and thoughtful stare.

"That is…" he drew out the 'is' while he searched for the word to follow it. "Fascinating. Fascinating? Yes, fascinating is what it is."

Patience was breathless with all that talking. "You don't think I'm mad? Seeing things no one else sees?"

He crooked one finger. "Come here." He pointed at the eyepiece of the telescope. "Look there."

Patience bent down. The brass tube pointed at a bright but tiny speck of light, midway from the horizon to the top of the sky. When she squinted through the lens, a large circle of light rushed into view. She gasped.

"It's got lines! Stripes! Fox in a bonnet! There are little dots all around it!"

"Moons," Linus said. "Like our own moon but around another world. And those stripes, I hypothesize, are clouds."

Patience stared, transfixed. She'd gazed up at the stars a thousand times but never guessed they could be like that.

"There's nothing mad about seeing things no one else sees," Linus said. "I do it all the time."

*Would it be rude to hug you?*

She decided she didn't care.

"Ooof!" he exclaimed, the wind knocked out of him by the vigor of her firm seizing.

When they separated, he cleared his throat a number of times. "Hrum. Right then. This is quite a mystery. Quite a mystery. We have much to discuss. Let's go—"

He stopped. He walked to the railing. He turned an ear to the night.

"What *is* that music?"

## 11. The Gabledancers

Sometimes you hear something without knowing it. When someone else points it out, all at once you realize the sound has been going on and on for a quite while and you can't help but wonder: "How could I have missed it?"

When Linus asked 'What *is* that music?' that same experience rushed over Patience. She joined him at the roof's edge. Together they listened hard into the night.

From somewhere below them — it was hard to pinpoint exactly the direction — pipes and drums and strings played a soft roundelay. The tune reminded Patience of a harvest fest, when everyone with so much as a toot-jug or plunk-harp to their name would gather in the fields and play their hearts out till the break of day.

"There!" Linus pointed down.

The hedges shivered far below. Odd, dark shapes slipped between them, limbs jerking in time to the music. Patience found herself tapping her foot, quite to her surprise. Out of the corner of her eye, she noticed Linus drumming the rails. Together, they swayed in rhythm.

The dancers in the garden converged on the house. They sprang from bush to bush. One of them leapt, up and up and impossibly up. He landed on the dome roof right above their heads! With a *snap* a tile broke loose under his foot and fell through the cupola, nearly cracking Patience's head with a great CRASH!

"Oi! Careful up there!"

A fiddle screeched. Silence filled the air.

The dark dancers far below crouched down. One by one, they sprung onto the Widow's Walk, landing with light little *tok tok toks*. Patience saw, to much concern, the whole pack of them were between her and Linus and both the ladder and the door!

"Do you know them?" Linus whispered.

"No."

The music started again, soft and slow. Instead of a wild celebration, the tune sounded cautious (to Patience's ears at least). She still hadn't seen a musician. She realized that, incredible as it seemed, the music was coming from the dancers — or from the dance.

The strangers jigged towards them in a line, two steps forward, one step back with a little kick in between each step.

"Goat-legs!" Linus gasped. He didn't sound scared. He sounded excited.

They *did* all have goat-legs, bent backwards and ending in hooves. From the waist up they had people-bodies. Their chests were bare under animal skin vests. She could not make out their faces.

The music sped up, as did the dancers. Their sharp little hooves sliced the air, closer and closer to Patience's head.

"Hey now!"

She clenched her fists and stepped in front of Linus. Her broom hung on its hook, too far away to do her any good. She wondered if he would mind if she used his telescope to whack their way to safety.

"Wait." He put a hand on her arm. "I'm curious to see where this goes."

She was going to say "Are you mad?!" She never got the chance. All of the dark dancers leaned in at once. A dozen gnarled hands with backwards thumbs seized them both. She was spun away from her friend, out into the center of the Widow's Walk. Through the tangle of waving limbs, she could see Linus was likewise surrounded.

The music changed once more. A deep drumbeat welled up from under the trilling tune. Without her wanting it to, Patience's foot tapped in time. Her knee jerked up and down.

"I say," she heard Linus call out. "Are you experiencing this same involuntary movement?"

"Yerp!" was all she could manage to reply. Her hands clapped. Her legs kicked and dipped. Her arms flung out wide as they could go.

A dancer grabbed each elbow. Three quick bounces and they hurled her into the air! She sailed up among the stars. At the zenith, she saw Linus, limbs akimbo.

"FLERGH!" Now he sounded scared.

They fell apart. She plummeted to earth, surrounded by sinuous shadows. Just before she was dashed to pieces on the roof tiles, they caught her. They set her down, gentle as an egg into a basket.

"Hu-hu-hu," Linus tried to say something. "Huhhhh...?"

"Don't worry," Patience said. "We're safe with them."

She had only meant to calm him down, but she found she believed her own words. It was mad as a clockwork cat in a tinker's dream, leaping around the steep-sloped roof. Just like a dream, though, the madness seemed right; there was music and dancing and who knows what else waiting in the wild, swirling night.

A boy-goat clattered up to her. Tiles cracked under his hoofs. He bowed.

Bemused, Patience curtsied, forgetting for a moment how precarious her perch was. She wobbled. The boy reached out a hand to steady her. The moment his hand touched hers, her feet became light and quick and as stable as on firm ground.

The boy-goat danced a three-step cavort. He motioned for her to try.

"Why not?" She was surprised at how easy it was, if she didn't think about it.

A girl-goat behind her cleared her throat. Patience turned round. The girl-goat held out her hand. Quick hoofs danced a more complicated six-step cavort. Patience matched her step for step, holding both the dancers' hands.

By the wide white glow of the Milky Way overhead, Patience could see them all clearly now. Their faces were wild and dangerous and kind and safe. They laughed with heedless joy. On the roof, their half-goat bodies weren't monstrous, but perfect and natural and right for the steep slope where they danced.

The boy-goat and girl-goat whirled Patience round the roof. Out of the corner of her eye, she could see a pair doing the same to Linus. They added steps, one at a time, till she lost count of the paces in a crazy complicated cavort. She couldn't tell whether she was leading them or they were leading her, whether the steps of the dance happened on their own or she chose each tip and tap of her toes. With the wind in her hair and music coming from everywhere, she couldn't care.

Without missing a beat, everyone jumped a grand jeté. They leapt off Pennywhack Manor at tremendous speed. The cobble streets flew by far, far below.

They landed on the peak of another roof. Patience passed hand-to-hand around the gable-dancing company. They jumped rooftop to rooftop across town. Here and there, a hoof broke a tile or punched through a patch of thatch, leaving a hole where the night air could flood into the house below.

Every now and then she clasped Linus, but the dance soon pulled them apart again. They'd lock eyes for the briefest moment. She knew he was thinking the same thing she was, deep down below the mad frenzy of the music on her mind. *Where are we going? Will we ever stop?*

The moon was low and rising by the time reason forced its way through the thrum of fiddles and drums.

The next time Patience was partnered with Linus, she held on. He nodded at her, taking her meaning in an instant.

*Time to go.*

They tried to escape the dance. The gabledancers would have none of it. Every time they took a step towards safety, one of the goat-folk blocked their way and spun them back to the group. It was all they could do to hang on to one another.

The music sped up and sped up and sped up again; frantic, mad, out-of-control. Their feet danced them on and on, over the roofs of Whosebourne toward who knew where.

With one last jump, they landed on the street. The fiddles screeched to a peak. The invisible musicians paused for a beat. One final discordant note sounded. All of the goat-folk stomped the ground at once. A great thunderous THWOK! echoed off into the silence of the night.

Between blinks, the dancers vanished up drainpipes and over gable edges. Patience and her new friend stood alone. The town bell sounded three sonorous tolls.

"Ri-hi-hi-hi," Linus stammered. "Th-heh-heh-heh-hen."

With that, he fainted.

## 12. The Marquis Goupil

To Patience's surprise, they were in the alley beside *The Crock and Dice*.

*Nice of the goats to dance me home.*

A little whiffling sound drifted up from the cobbles. Linus lay, still out cold, at her feet. Miss Alys kept smelling salts in a drawer. She headed inside to fetch them.

The kitchen door stood ajar. Patience's heart dropped to her stomach faster than a tile falling from a roof under a goaty hoof. A burglar could be robbing the inn!

She scuttled inside. She shut the door behind her with as quiet a *click* as she could. She seized and brandished her broom. If there were a thief, she'd make him regret stealing from her place.

She took stock of the kitchen in the low red light of the sleeping fire. Nothing big was missing. She checked the cabinets with the dishes and every silver drawer. Nothing small was missing either. Relieved (and forgetting for a moment about the smelling salts), she sat on a stool and sighed.

*Scritch-scratch... scritch-scratch... snuff-snuff... scratch-scritch... whump... scruff... scruff... scruff...*

The sounds came from behind the pantry curtain.

One careful step at a time, Patience crept towards the intruder.

Just as she was about to throw the curtain aside and yell AHA! a small animal pushed its way out.

A fox! In the inn!

He did not notice her. He tugged a side of dried beef awkwardly along the kitchen floor, towards the alley door, *scruff... scruff...*

Patience hesitated. She should shoo the beast out. But she didn't want to raise a ruckus and wake everyone up.

For his part, the fox acted as if he were perfectly within his rights to abscond with a side of Miss Alys' beef. He reached the alley door. He dropped the pilfered meat. He cocked his head at the now-closed exit.

He glanced at Patience. He poked his snout twice at the door.

She took the hint.

"Alright," she whispered. "But be quiet."

Better to lose a side of beef than have to explain how the fox got inside in the first place, or what she was doing up at three in the morning.

He waited for her to let him out. His thick black tail wrapped round the whole of his lower body. He looked quite distinguished. Patience put up her broom and opened the door.

He stretched low on his front legs, almost as if he were bowing. He picked up his treat. He brushed Patience's skirts as he left.

Once out in the alley, he dropped the beef again. He turned back to her. He was the picture of innocence — if she ignored the stolen meat at his feet. He crinkled his snout like a smirk. He opened his mouth.

"No," Patience said. "Absolutely not. Not talking animals. I won't have it."

"As you wish, my dear," the fox said in a most sophisticated accent. "Should I just be on my way, then?"

She was so tired. Dancing all night on the roofs with goat-folk and now this. Her bed lay just behind her, down the dark hall in a nice dark room where she could sleep at least two hours.

She stepped outside and sat down on the stoop.

"A wise choice," the fox purred. "Curiosity, as they say, may have killed the cat. But satisfaction, no, it brought her back?"

"A fox," Patience muttered. "No bonnet though."

He offered her a courteous paw, which she took. "You have the pleasure of addressing the Marquis Goupil. And you are, of course, the celebrated Mademoiselle Patience Fell, of whom all the Chaos-Court-in-Exile chatters these days."

Linus, whom Patience had clear forgotten, sat bolt upright.

"Exile?"

The Marquis leapt all-four-feet off the ground, fur a-bristle.

"Stand and deliver!" he said as he landed. "I'll demand challenge, if you threaten this girl."

Patience couldn't help but notice that he'd positioned himself not between her and Linus, but between Linus and the side of beef.

"It's fine," she said to the fox, kneeling next to her friend. "Are you alright?"

"Quite." Linus tried to smoothe his hair but just mussed it in the other direction. "Assuming the fox is, in fact, talking."

"He is."

The Marquis sniffed the air up and down. "Master Pennywhack? I had not expected to find you out and about twixt Witching Hour and dawn."

"Have we met, sir?"

"If we had, would you need to ask that question?"

Linus furrowed his brow. "I suppose not. But how —"

"—do I know who you are? My dear boy, as the ranking member of the Chaos-Court-in-Exile, it's my business to know who's who in Whosebourne." The fox blinked. "Listen to me. I sound like an owl. How gauche."

"So it's you in charge of the offaltosser?" Patience regretted leaving her broom in the kitchen.

The Marquis gave a noble little chuckle. "Rank hath its responsibilities, and sometimes the responsibilities are rank." He nosed the side of beef with the greatest tact. "You don't mind if I —?"

"Go ahead."

"Many thanks. No need to be uncivilized." He nibbled the beef, speaking between bites. He swallowed every bite all the way, very proper, before each new sentence.

"Yes, it is true that I am, in a distant way, 'in charge' of the offaltosser. The more distance the better. I don't begrudge you the whack-work though. It made quite the witty story. Oh!" he interrupted himself. "My pardons, but you simply must try this. It is delicious. Exquisite, even."

"No, thank you."

"Are you certain? Very well. Where was I?"

"You said —" Linus said at the same time as Patience asked: "Why —?"

Linus bowed while sitting. "You first."

"Thank you."

"An admirable display of chivalry, Master Pennywhack," the Marquis said. "But unnecessary. Your two questions are sides of a coin."

Linus furrowed his brow even deeper. In the moonlight, he looked as wrinkled as a hundred-year-old man. "How could you possibly know what we were going to ask?"

"A bagatelle." The Marquis waved a paw. "One of the advantages of my lofty place in the world is the perspective it affords. Also—and it will save a great deal of time if you remember this—I am very, very, clever." He thought about it. "Add a few more verys."

"Brmphm."

"You, Demoiselle Fell," the Marquis continued, ignoring Linus' skeptical grunt, "are doubtless wondering 'why me?'"

He pressed one paw to his chest in a deprecating moue.

"'To what quality do I, a mere broom-girl, owe these visits from the Fair Folk, both lofty'," (he arched a smug eyebrow), "'and lowest of the low. Why me?'"

In fact, that was not what she was going to ask. She had been going to ask if he was so fancy, why was he stealing beef from a low-rent inn like a common thief?

The question 'Why me?' made very little sense to her. Things happened how they happened to whomever they happened to. But he was a talking fox and had a title, so she humored him.

"Alright. Why me then?"

"At first, just chance. That's the way everything begins. You happened to veer from the street into an alley at the same moment the offaltosser was doing the stinky things he does. But in that happenstance encounter, you stood your ground, most bravely. Knight of the broom, I'd entitle you, were it up to me to hand out titles."

Patience felt sure she was being mocked. The Marquis went on.

"Not only did you display prowess in the art of combat, but afterwards, you knelt down and cared for your fallen foe."

"What else would I do? I was the one who knocked him silly. I should be the one to make sure he got back up."

"You might be surprised how rare that sentiment is," Linus murmured.

"Quite." The Marquis finished the last bite of his treat. "When I heard the tale of the town's latest broom-girl, I knew you were someone to keep an eye on. My confidence has been rewarded. Every step of the way you've shown pluck and derring-do. You barely blinked at the cobblemaulers. You scampered up the side of Pennywhack Manor like a squirrel up a—"

"—What?" Linus interjected.

"I'll tell you later," Patience replied.

"And, when I sent the gabledancers to fetch you, I find to my surprise, you've even recruited an ally."

Linus objected with another *brmphm*. "In point of fact, sir, it was I who—"

"Hush," Patience said. "Let him finish." Then, to the Marquis: "Why did you do all this? You must want something."

The fox tapped the side of his snout. "You're as focused as a hawk over a rabbit, Demoiselle. Yes. I do require your services. As to what I need: the answer to that lies in young Master Pennywhack's question."

"You said the Chaos Court was in exile, inexilebywhomandfromwhere?" Linus asked, his words spilling over one another in his haste to get his question out before the Marquis could ask it for him.

The fox pressed a paw to his forehead. "Yes, woe! I and my few followers are all that remains in this world of the Chaos Court. The rest are banished to the Who-Knows-Where. And we are powerless to free them. But you—"

"—Me? You expect *me* to do something about it?" Patience didn't care for his melodramatic attitude. "So more of you can wreck up the town?"

Goupil waved his other paw. "Hardly. Not a bit of it. Never happen. When the King and Queen return—"

A slipper flew from the darkness above them, narrowly missing him.

Crowquill leaned out her attic window. She held a second shoe, ready to throw.

"A gentleman," the Marquis said, "does not overstay his welcome."

He bowed like a playful dog. His teeth flashed in the light of the new-risen moon. "See you soon, Demoiselle Fell."

Crowquill's other slipper hurtled down into the alley, but the fox had scampered into the night when it hit.

## 13. Patience Ponders Her Place in the World

"Right then." Linus pushed himself to his feet. He strode cross the alley. He picked up one of Crowquill's slippers. To Patience's shock, he held it to his face and took a deep sniff.

"Smells like foot."

He nodded, like he'd proved something.

"Yes...? Shouldn't it?" She wondered if he'd hit his head when the gabledancers had dropped them off.

"I've never had a dream with smell," he said. "Have you?"

She'd never thought about it. "I guess not."

He explained further. "I just danced with goat-people across every roof in town and conversed with a talking fox who claims to be a noble in something called the Chaos Court. A dream seemed the most likely explanation, so I wanted to rule it out."

"I suppose that makes sense," Patience said. "But did you have to sniff the slipper? The alley trash is pretty whiff all on its own."

"Oh." He lowered the shoe. "Um, yes, certainly—but I thought—that is to say—I—I—" He trailed off stammering. Even in the moonlight she could tell he was blushing something fierce.

"It was smart to double-check."

He coughed. "At any rate. Not to change the subject, but it is getting quite late. I shouldn't be out of the manor by the time it gets light. We have a great deal to discuss and even more to figure out, but I'm afraid it will have to wait."

He pressed the slipper into her hands. He stepped back. He bowed. "Miss Fell. Good evening and hope to see you soon."

With that, Patience was alone in the alley once again.

*Isn't that just fine.* She hunted around for Crowquill's other shoe. *What now?*

The attic window was closed. The light was still on. Patience didn't have it in her to deal with Crowquill's rambling, rhyming non-answers. It had been a long night.

She retrieved the other shoe. She went inside and made her way to bed. She stuffed both slippers next to *The Chaos Court*. Resting her head on the last tiny sliver of pillow that wasn't lumped up by Crowquill's cast-offs, she settled in to sleep.

It didn't take.

As weary as her bones were, her brain was still abuzz. Every weird thing since Linus snuck into her kitchen that morning tumbled round and round in her head, making a dreadful racket.

She tried sorting it all out. Maybe if she could do that her brain would quiet down so she could sleep.

*Why me?*

The Marquis had put the question in her head. It still didn't make much sense. As he'd said, she just happened along. She needed a place in the world, *The Crock and Dice* needed a girl with a broom.

But everything after that...

The fox was the key. He wanted her to do something about the rest of the Chaos Court. But she didn't believe for a second if more of his friends came to Whosebourne it would be a good thing.

On the other hand, she had no reason to think it wouldn't be a good thing. The gabledancers had frightened her at first and they turned out to be fine. A bit wild, but fine. Maybe if she helped the Marquis out, the offaltossers and cobblemaulers would stop wrecking things. Maybe that's what the King and Queen were for, to keep them under control.

Then there was the Keyreeve. He knew something was going on. He wouldn't have ordered her to keep quiet otherwise. Still, it was hard to believe he knew all about the Marquis and the others. He didn't seem clever enough.

Clever or not, he had the power to lock her in the stocks all day or worse if she stepped in the wrong cow pie.

And the whole town was littered with wrong cow pies.

*UGH!* She flipped over and punched the pillow.

*All I wanted was to find my place in the world. I'm twelve, everyone says 'it's time to find your place in the world.' So I did. I found* The Crock and Dice *and I worked hard every day to learn a trade. That's supposed to be that. Find your place, stick to it, grow up, and call it a day.*

*Instead, I'm all mixed up with Kings and Queens and Keyreeves and their nephews and talking foxes and crazy attic ladies and impossible creatures with silly names who are tearing this whole town apart and no one believes me except one wheezy boy with crooked glasses and no one will help and I can't figure out what anyone wants from me or what I'm supposed to do about any of it and if I do the wrong thing it will go badly for me and there might not even be a right thing to do!*

*I'm in over my head. More than in over my head.*

Patience silently sang a song her father would sing in just such moments:

*I'm down at the bottom of a well*
*and it's cold and the night is coming in*
*and the rain is pouring down and the water's rising up*
*and I don't know how to swim.*

Then he'd clap twice and begin again. Over and over, faster and faster, until the words couldn't keep up with the tune and his troubles ran gasping away.

The song whirled round her brain till her thoughts couldn't keep up. She opened her eyes. Miss Alys whiffled a little snore. The moon had set. By the smell of the air and the sound of the town, there was an hour to go till dawn.

*Enough of this nonsense. None of the other broom-girls stayed. Why should I?*

She got up. She gathered her few clothes and wrapped them tight into a blanket-bindle. She considered leaving a note to say goodbye. She decided not to.

*You haven't been here that long*, she told herself. *They won't even miss you a day from now. Someone else can clean up their messes.*

She stopped in the kitchen to tie the bindle to her broom. She looked round *The Crock and Dice* one last time.

"I thought you were my place in the world," she whispered to the empty inn. "I guess I was wrong."

Her eyes burned. She scuffed them with the back of her wrist.

Alone in the street, she couldn't decide where to go. She wanted so badly to go back home. But her feet wouldn't move towards the country road. She pictured her mother and father, seeing her come home so soon. They would be so disappointed. They would make room, of course, but there had never really been enough room.

She had heard stories about going off to sea. Maybe she could find her place somewhere among the waves and fish, sweeping the deck of a fast-rushing ship.

A scrap of paper blew by like a tiny white sail on the blue morning breeze. Patience raised her broom, ready for more.

It was only a stray bit of trash; not an offaltosser in sight.

What if one showed up after she left? Miss Alys wouldn't have anyone to broom-whack it away.

And what if the cook took a carriage ride and crashed in a cobblemauler hole? She wasn't very spry and she could get very hurt! What if she was outside and the gabledancers kicked a roof-tile crashing down onto her head?

What if something worse came to Whosebourne, a piece of the Chaos Court Patience hadn't even seen?

There would be no one to stop them. There would be no one to keep Miss Alys safe.

*But I don't know if I can keep her safe. I don't know how to fix any of it. There's just me against all of it.*

The sky brightened all around. Most of the stars were gone. A single bright spot shone near the western horizon, undimmed by the rising sun. Patience remembered its moons and clouds, invisible to the ordinary eye. She remembered the boy atop the Widow's Walk who showed her there was more to the stars than she had ever imagined.

Linus. He was all alone too. He believed her. He wanted to help.

How could he help, with his wheezy breathing and big words? He would probably faint if he tried to swat an offaltosser.

No. He wasn't strong. But he was clever. And maybe, with her being strong and him being clever, it would be enough.

She wasn't alone.

She had help and she had someone who needed her help.

*Maybe there's not much more of a place in the world than that.*

She went back inside. She untied the bindle from her broom and got an early start on the sweeping up.

## 14. Back to Pennywhack Manor

On her next day off (because even broom-girls don't work *all* the time), Patience went straight to see Linus.

She scrubbed her hands and her face till they shone. She put on her least-messy dress (she only had two, but that was enough for one to be cleaner than the other). She tucked Crowquill's copy of *The Chaos Court* under her arm and set off through Whosebourne at a brisk pace.

In no time at all, she stood beneath the gleaming walls of Pennywhack Manor. Or rather, she stood on the far side of the iron fence that surrounded the grounds in front of the gleaming walls of Pennywhack Manor.

She marched up.

Coinquaff wasn't on duty. In his place, a young man in a stiff uniform stood on the other side of the fence. Sweat glistened on his pimply face. His narrow rounded shoulders were pulled back hard by his coat. He reminded Patience of a sheep in the shearing pen. If it weren't for the starch in his coat, she felt sure he'd have slouched off to find a nap in the grass.

"Sir," she called out. "I'm here to see Linus, sir."

The guard stirred. "Wot?"

Patience repeated herself.

He bleared down his spotty nose with half-lidded eyes. "You?"

"Sir, yes, sir."

He curled up one side of his wispy-whiskered upper lip. "No."

"That's it? Just no?"

He hitched his shoulders awkwardly — as though he were trying to shrug, but the starch in his coat wouldn't let him.

"Fishl bidness ernly."

It took her a moment to translate that into 'official business only.'

"I am on official business," she said. "Linus will tell you."

"Li'us?" He snerked at the thought of a broom-girl knowing the Keyreeve's nephew.

Patience wasn't so easily put off. "What about Reynard? Can I see him?"

"Hrf hrf hrf," the snobby boy emitted a starch-stifled laugh.

"Oi!"

She wished she had her broom so she could jab him in the short ribs through the fence-bars.

This was getting her nowhere. Reynard or Linus or *somebody* had to come or go sometime. When they did, the gate would open. She could outrun the starched-up guard without trying.

"I'll wait."

"Stchrsf," the guard said, somehow turning 'suit yourself' into a one-syllable word.

It didn't take long for her to get tired of waiting. The more she thought about it, running through the gate when someone proper came in was a bad idea. Getting chased around the house by gate guards wasn't the proper way to visit a friend.

The spiked iron fence disappeared into hedges on her left and right. The hedges ran far as she could see.

*Maybe there's another way in.*

Trying to look like she was out for a casual stroll, she scouted along the perimeter of the Pennywhack grounds.

Here and there in breaks in the shrubbery, she caught a peek of the fence. Its bars were too narrow to squeeze through. She could easily have climbed it, but the spikes on the top looked wicked dangerous to cross.

Red fur flashed in the corner of her eye. A bushy black tail disappeared into the hedges a ways ahead.

"Marquis!" she called. The hedges rustled and swayed.

She sprinted to where the fox had disappeared. There, the branches had been bent into an arc. Beneath that, a deep burrow ran under the fence.

Patience checked all round. By luck, the street was clear.

She slipped *The Chaos Court* through the bars of the fence, resting it on a crook of branches. She dove head-first into the foxhole. She squirmed and squeezed through the wormy wet earth, getting her hands and face and her least-messy dress covered in mud.

She crawled out the other side. If she'd been much more grown, she never would have made it. She scanned round for the Marquis Goupil. He was nowhere to be found.

She stood in a secluded part of the grounds. An old stone shed, with cracked glass windows held together by decades of dirt, blocked her view of the main house. On her other side, the thicket continued, snarled and untended. A grey gravel path, shot through with weeds, ran beneath her feet and around the shed.

"Marquis?" she whispered. "Sir? Marquis Goupil?"

No reply. Not even the scritch-scratch of claws on gravel. The hedges didn't move an inch.

*It was just a regular old fox,* she told herself. *You remember what a fox is, don't you? You're all turned round by this mad town.*

Regardless, she was where she wanted to be. Time to find Linus.

Stepping quiet as a cat after a barn mouse, she followed the path to the edge of the shed. She peeked round.

"Oh!" she cried, when she saw who was there.

"GAH!" cried Reynard, who had been leaning up against the building eating a sandwich.

"Splunch," went the sandwich as it hit the gravel.

"Aw!" Reynard stared at his ruined lunch. "That's a sad thing."

"I'm so sorry!" Patience picked up the beef and bread. She did her best to brush them off. Her hands were so dirty from crawling under the fence, she only made things worse.

"Never mind." Reynard took the shattered sandwich from her. "Not every mess can be cleaned up."

He tossed it into a nearby bin. He bowed.

"Farewell, roast beef. You were delicious. Exquisite, even."

"Are you going to tell the guard I snuck in?"

Reynard barked a loud laugh. Several startled crows burst from a nearby tree. Cawing angry crow-words at him, they flew off over the house.

"That spotty stuffed sausage? Not a bit of it. Not my department. Come and go as you please, I say."

Patience sighed in relief.

"I assume," Reynard said with a sly smile, "that you're here to see Linus?"

"Is that alright?"

"Of course! I admire your resourcefulness. And, while his uncle may disagree, between you and me, the boy is a bit too isolated for his own good." He tapped the side of his nose. "Still, discretion is the watchword."

Patience curtsied. "Sir, yes, sir," she said in a friendly, happy way, without a trace of servant in her voice. She decided that, for all his sarcastic ways, she rather liked Reynard after all.

"Onward then." Reynard stepped off down the path.

"Wait!" She ran back to the fence and retrieved *The Chaos Court* from the hedges.

As she caught up with him, Reynard eyed the enormous volume. "A little light reading?"

"Linus wanted to borrow it."

"How kind of you," he said and led her into the house.

## 15. Linus' Place in the World

What Patience saw from the doorway to Linus' room stopped her dead in her tracks.

"Fox in a bonnet with a velvet suit," she whispered, quite taken aback.

She had no idea there were that many books in the world. Even the schoolhouse back home didn't have a tenth that many.

"Beg pardon?" Reynard murmured over her shoulder. "Fox in a what?"

She shook her head to say 'never mind' and went on into the room.

She couldn't believe anyone could read that many books. Crammed shelves rose floor-to-ceiling on every wall. There were books of every size, bound in all the colors of the rainbow. She could tell they were neatly organized, but how, she hadn't a clue.

She noted with approval that there wasn't a speck of dust on them.

Linus had his back to her. He stared, absorbed, at a large slate board covered in squiggly symbols she couldn't make head nor tail of.

"Assuming the impetus iota," he muttered, tapping a piece of chalk on his cheek, "and allowing for an aetherial drag coefficient of… hrm…"

Patience wondered whether he might not be a wizard after all.

Reynard attempted to interrupt Linus' deliberations with a delicate cough.

"Just a moment." Linus held up one chalk-dusty hand.

More than a moment went by and he showed no signs of turning round.

"I'll leave you to it." Reynard withdrew.

While Linus mumbled weird words and made arcane marks on the board, Patience took in the rest of his place.

Two large tables filled the middle of the room. On one sat many glass display boxes. Half of them contained rocks and half contained dead bugs. Each item, rock or bug, bore a label written in a tiny, neat hand.

The other table held a set of odd-shaped pots connected by glass tubes. A low blue flame glowed under one of the pots. Green liquid bubbled in spurts through a tube and dripped into a carafe of purple crystals.

*Yep,* Patience thought. *Wizard.*

She wasn't too worried about him doing anything wizardly-bad though. Reynard wouldn't have left her alone if that had been a likely thing.

She'd never seen a wizard work. There was no doubt that Linus was working, even though he stood stock-still. His shoulders hunched like he carried two bushels of wheat straight from harvest. His face scrunched hard. He wheezed like he'd run five miles 'cross hill and dale to chase down a loose greased pig.

Patience had never seen anyone struggle so hard while not doing anything.

He'd said he was from the country. She tried to imagine him raising ruckus with the rough-and-tumble boys back home. It was impossible. He wasn't like anyone she'd ever met. Standing in the middle of his room, surrounded by his books and squiggles and rocks and bugs, she felt entirely out of place.

What had she been thinking, coming all this way to bother him? He'd probably forgotten all about the Chaos Court for some more interesting wizard problem. She opened the door to leave.

Suddenly, Linus hurled his chalk at the board and heaved an angry HRM!

"It doesn't make any sense! No matter what value I assign for the aetherial coefficient, it's too high. Everything should grind to a halt. What do you think, Reynard?"

He turned round.

"Oh!" His scrunched-up face danced into a smile. "Patience Fell!"

When he smiled and said her name, she didn't feel quite so out of place.

"Hello." She closed the door again.

Smoothing his tousled hair, he bustled over to her. "Oh my. I h-had no idea you were there. H-how l-long have you been there?"

"I—"

"—T-terribly sorry to be so rude. I didn't know you were there."

"It's alri—"

"—I wouldn't want you to think I go around ignoring people. I was working and I didn't know—"

"—that I was here," Patience interrupted. "It's fine."

"Oh. Yes. Well." He smoothed his hair some more, even though it no longer needed it. "Right then. Quite fine."

He moved on to straightening his shirt, fussing with it all out of proportion. Patience couldn't help but smile at how flustered he was. He noticed and blushed.

"So," she said, casting about for something to fill the awkward silence. "You came from the country?"

"Yes I did!" His eyes took on a faraway look. Patience knew how he felt.

"My family," he continued, "has, for the past two hundred years, maintained an estate in Whackshire."

*Estate.* That explained it. She had an aunt in service at an estate — she said it was as fancy as the town.

"You're from the country as well, of course."

*It's not the same,* she wanted to say, but instead she nodded.

"Come to town to seek your place in the world, like me?"

"You've got to find your place in the world too?"

"It," he looked serious, "found me."

He clasped his hands behind his back like a schoolmaster. "The proper place for a Pennywhack is in government. And the proper place for the eldest Pennywhack of each generation," he recited, dull as a summer lesson, "is to be Keyreeve. To that end, I am to learn the arts of politics, governance, regulations, management, and above all, bureaucracy, in order that, when the time comes, I may take my uncle's position as leader of Whosebourne."

"Sounds important."

"It's ghastly."

Patience didn't know what to say to that. She'd never thought being fancy could be such a trial.

"But enough of that," Linus clapped his hands and rubbed them together. "For now, my uncle is content to ignore me most of the day. Which means I can do as I please. Like my experiments."

The pots of green liquid burbled in happy agreement.

Patience finally felt comfortable enough to broach the touchy subject. "Are you a wizard?"

"BWAH!" Linus guffawed. "W-w-wizz…" he tried to say, but lost his words to a wheezing 'heheheh.'

"I'm serious!" She glared. She did not like being made fun of.

"S-sorry." He took off his glasses and wiped tears from his eyes. "No. I am not a wizard."

"Then what's with the spells?" She jabbed a finger at the board. "And the potions? And… and…" she gesticulated at the bugs and rocks under glass, "whatever those are for."

He pointed at the board. "Physics." He pointed at the pots and then the collections. "Chemistry, entomology, and geology."

"Hrmph. Wizard words." She crossed her fingers behind her back in case he was going to cast a spell on her.

Linus composed himself. "I'm sorry for laughing. I wasn't laughing at you, I promise. It's just that, ermhem,

I find wizards ridiculous. I," he puffed his chest out a little, "am a scientist."

"I don't know what that is." Once more she felt far, far out of place.

"A wizard muddles the world with mysteries," he explained. "And confuses everyone to make them afraid."

"I'm not afraid."

"Of course you're not. You're brave. Maybe the bravest person I've ever met"

Miss Alys, Crowquill, and the Marquis Goupil had all called her that. But it didn't mean much coming from them. Coming from Linus, it ruffled her whole mind like a week's laundry blown off the line.

"A scientist," he continued, "elucidates the truth with experiments and makes things clearer than they were before. The clearer things are, the less afraid people will be."

"I suppose."

"Speaking of which! You came here with that book. I have a lot of questions about the Chaos Court. I haven't forgotten our midnight dance. Let's figure this mess out together, shall we?"

He held out his hand. She shook it. Wizard or scientist, he was her friend. The lonely feeling of out-of-place vanished like a green bubble popping over a blue fire.

# 16. Crowquill's Curious Book

Careful not to jostle the boiling pots, Patience crossed to the desk while Linus bustled next door. He returned with a second chair. They sat side-by-side and considered Crowquill's copy of *The Chaos Court* by Johnny Factotum.

Patience moved to open it.

"Wait." Linus put his hand on hers. "Let's see what we can learn from the outside, before diving in."

He leaned in very close to the book. He peered at it, tipping his spectacles to the bridge of his nose. He sniffed the leather binding. He thumped it with his index finger. He pressed his ear to the cover and thumped it again. He traced the silver letters of the title.

He sat back. "It's at least two hundred years old."

"How do you know that?"

"By seeing what isn't there."

Patience snorted. "I've had quite enough of that, thank you very much."

"Oh? You've been seeing things that aren't there?"

"No, it's just—." He was so serious. She let the joke go. "Never mind. How do you know it's old?"

He pushed his glasses back with his index finger. "It lacks a Stamp of Approval."

"What's that?"

"All books published since the Keyreeves became leaders of Whosebourne have to be stamped with a little key-shape, pushed into the leather. That means the book has been officially approved."

"Hrmph." Patience pictured the brubaing Keyreeve deciding what people could and couldn't read. She didn't like the notion one bit.

"It's the custom," Linus said with a shrug. "For two hundred years."

"What about before that?"

"Before the Keyreeves, Whosebourne was led by a Lord Mayor. Aldo Pennywhack, my many-greats-grandfather, established the office of Keyreeve after the last Lord Mayor resigned."

"Why'd he do that?"

"You know, I've never thought about it. It's what the history books say happened. They don't say why."

"The history books that have to be approved by the Keyreeves?"

"Hrm. I see what you're saying."

He took a sheet of blank paper from a neat pile on the desk. He dipped his silver-nibbed pen in the inkwell and wrote:

*Lord Mayor to Keyreeve – why? (Real history? Possible connection to Chaos Court?)*

"It may not relate," he explained, "but this is the only book I've ever seen in my uncle's vicinity. It means something secret to him. He objected strongly when I asked to borrow it after you'd left."

"Brubarubaruba." Patience shook out her cheeks like grumpy jowls.

Linus half-stifled a surprise snicker. He composed himself—mostly. "Quite. An accurate recreation of the conversation."

He opened the book to the title page.

"The Chaos Court by Johnny Factotum," he read aloud. He made a note:

*J. Factotum – Who?*

"So you don't know him?"

"No."

She pointed at the shelves and shelves of books. "That's saying something."

"Those? Not much to speak of," Linus said. "There are buildings twice the size of this house, stacked with books four stories high."

"Pft. You're having me on."

"No, it's true! But we're getting distracted." He turned the page.

A large picture spanned the next two pages.

"This appears to be a woodcut print of the old style." Linus scratched notes as he made observations. "It portrays a town scene, populated by dozens and dozens of common people and creatures of unusual anatomy."

"At the bottom there, it says 'The Chaos Court'! There's the cobblemauler—see his friend coming out of the rock in the street? And that squiggle-squoggle with the bits of paper and fishbones must be the offaltosser."

"Fascinating. And on this rooftop here are the goat-footed people. I presume those lines around their arms and legs are meant to indicate dancing."

"There are so many different ones."

"Indeed." Linus counted under his breath. His nib dipped and scribbled at a furious pace.

Patience didn't know which of the marvelous Fair Folk to inspect first. Her eyes were drawn to a tiny speck of a butterfly-man, who had enormous hands instead of wings. His fingers and thumb pinched towards an ordinary woman on the opposite page, whose necklace was flying right off her neck.

*He don't look up to any good.*

Not all the plain folk in the scene were being pranked by creatures of the Chaos Court. But most were.

A boy chased his chamberpot across the street as a wee man-shaped swarm of roaches, all working together, absconded with it. Judging by the boy's cross-legged gait, he really, really needed it back.

A merchant grabbed at apples flying everywhere as a mischievous imp upended his cart.

Near that, two scholars in black gowns went at each other all fisticuffs. Patience guessed they'd been goaded into an argument by the two wee mouths-with-hands that clung to their flaring ears.

"What a royal mess," she muttered.

"Where *are* they?" Linus tapped his pen on his cheek, leaving a black smudge.

"Whosebourne?"

"I don't think so. It could be, but remember the Marquis Goupil said there were only a few of his people in town. He called them the 'Chaos-Court-in-Exile.'"

"Right! What does that mean?"

"Exile means they've been sent away from home."

"To find their place in the world?"

"Not quite. It's more of a punishment. Imagine you had to leave both the country and Whosebourne and go somewhere else."

"Is there anywhere else?"

Linus laughed. "Quite right, quite right."

She hadn't been joking. Now she felt stupid; an ignorant country clod who quit school at twelve to find her place and didn't go but a few months each year till then. Her face burned. She stared hard at the book.

"Oh." Linus figured it out. "I'm sorry. I thought—that is…"

He stood up. "That was most rude of me. I apologize. Yes, there are many, many places in this world." He went to his shelves. "I'll show you, in one of my atlases."

"No!"

"Are you sure?"

"Forget that. Forget it all." She'd seen something that banished her hurt feelings. She stabbed the woodcut with her finger. "Look at this!"

There was a ramshackle building with a wild-haired woman leaning out of its attic—reaching for a crow. Sheaves of paper cascaded from the window to the street below. There, a grinning fox gathered them up in his mouth, about to run away.

"That's Miss Crowquill," Patience whispered.

"The woman in the attic who owns this book?"

She nodded. It was the same person. Not a relative or ancestor. The very same woman she'd delivered breakfast to, her first morning in town. The spit and image of the odd bird who'd chanted weird rhymes at her and knew all about the Chaos Court and had given her this book.

"Two hundred years..."

"And yet," Linus said, his voice hushed, "there she is."

Wheezing (with excitement or fear, Patience couldn't tell), he scratched another note.

*Crowquill's possibly immortal. And possibly one of Them.*

They were so caught up in contemplating that twist, they didn't notice the Keyreeve come in.

## 17. Reynard's Lesson

"BRUBARUBARUBA!"

"AH!" the children cried in unison and jumped to their feet.

The Keyreeve's beet-red face wobbled inches from them. Three paces behind him stood Reynard. The servant had a serious face, but when he caught Patience's eye, he gave her a sympathetic twitch of his shoulders.

"Uncle... Miss Fell... was just..." That was all Linus could manage. He struggled to catch his breath.

"I know exactly what this *servant* was doing," the Keyreeve rumbled. His jowls shook like a bull about to charge. Reynard rolled his eyes a smidge.

Patience stuck her chin back at the brubaing man. "And what's that I'm doing?" she demanded. "Lying? Like you told me to?"

"BWA! BRUB! WHAB!" The Keyreeve choked as if all the words he knew charged up towards his mouth at once and got stuck in his throat on the way.

Linus kept on gasping for air.

"Sir, perhaps I could be of help, sir." Reynard sounded as if he doubted it.

"Unconsciously fresh!" the Keyreeve exclaimed, finding his words. Almost.

"Unconscionably, sir," Reynard corrected.

The Keyreeve whirled on his red-coated assistant. "What was that?!"

"Nothing sir." Reynard coughed delicately. "A tickle in my throat."

The Keyreeve turned back to the children. Linus gripped the side of his desk, still wheezing like a calf with the croup.

"Unconsciously fresh, girl!" the Keyreeve thundered, sticking to his mistake. "I ordered you not to spread your silly country superstitions! Bad enough you stir up every Sally Sweepstoop and Mickey Muckstall in the lower orders. But to come into a gentleman's house and ply his foolish nephew with such frippery is beyond the Pale. I've a good mind—"

Reynard arched one eyebrow. He mouthed 'A good mind?'

Patience snerked.

The Keyreeve ceased his bluster. His eyes narrowed. They glittered viciously. The only sound in the room was Linus, sucking wind. The bull was about to charge.

When he spoke again, he was very, very quiet.

"Reynard. Take this *filthy* country girl back to her place in the *dirt* and see that she stays there. If I find her again on my property, I want her whipped and I want her jailed."

It wasn't until the Keyreeve sneered the words 'filthy' and 'dirt' that Patience realized she was still muddy from crawling under the Pennywhack fence. Linus hadn't said a thing about it. But she was a pig in a wallow amid all those fancy things. She stared down at her clunky country shoes, covered in brown clots, shedding onto the rich carpet.

The Keyreeve was right.

She was very far away from her proper place in the world.

Her face burned. Shame punched her in the chest and gripped her heart in an iron fist. She flinched when Reynard touched her arm. She fled through the door without his help.

"Miss Fell," Linus croaked.

"SILENCE!"

Patience could hear the Keyreeve shout on and on, even after she and Reynard were well down the hall.

"You presume too much, boy! You need discipline! I'll start by confiscating this ridiculous book and the rest of this — this — whatever this nonsense is!"

After that, Patience couldn't make out the rest of the Keyreeve's rant, but it went on and on. His voice thundered after her, down the stairs, through the servants' halls behind the fancy walls, out the side of the manor house, and past the stiff and cruelly snobbish guard at the gate.

She was well away from Pennywhack Manor, down streets she didn't even remember stalking through, when she noticed Reynard was still walking beside her.

"What are you doing here?" she asked, not slowing down. "Isn't your place back with the Brubarubarubareeve?"

"That ham-in-a-sock?" Reynard sniffed dismissively. "Not on my day off, it isn't. I only happened onto the scene when he was about to discover you and I couldn't sto —"

"Why don't you leave me be?!" Patience whirled left at a corner. Reynard followed her down a new street, without missing a beat.

" — p him from opening the door. A few seconds earlier, and —"

Patience didn't care. She just wanted to be alone with her shame. "Go away! You and your fancy coat and fancy manners and fancy words. You don't want to get any dirt on yourself from someone dirty like me."

Reynard's only reply was to keep walking by her side.

She tried to ignore him. She tried to ignore everyone on the street. She felt very small and enormous all at once, like no one could see her but everyone was staring all the same.

As strong a walker as she was, Patience couldn't keep up that pace forever. When she got to the empty Fairgate Square, she stopped and dropped to the curb. She scrubbed her face hard with the back of her hand. She was surprised to find her cheeks were very wet.

"Great," she muttered, "on top of everything, I cried in front of everyone in town."

Reynard hunkered down in front of her. He cocked his head to the side, concern in his eyes. For an odd moment, with his deep black pants and fox red coat, he reminded her of the Marquis Goupil. She didn't want to think about any of that, so she stared over his shoulder at the strange iron gate to nowhere in the middle of the square.

"An unpleasant lesson, Patience Fell," he said softly. "I'm not sorry you had to learn it, though. Better sooner than later."

"What lesson is that?"

He slapped the thighs of his black trousers and stood up. He clasped his hands behind the tails of his long red coat. As he talked, he strode back and forth like Linus did when he was lecturing. Not that she'd ever see that again.

"There are two kinds of people in this world," Reynard began. "There are the people like Linus and the Keyreeve who live in big houses and have things done for them. The People in the Fancy Halls, let's call them."

Patience didn't think Linus was anything like the Keyreeve. But she didn't correct Reynard. Her attention was distracted by a crow, who had just fluttered to the ground across the square.

"And then there are people like you and me, who live in little rooms, out of sight, and do things for our betters." He snickered at the word 'betters'. "We do things for them, so they don't have to do anything for themselves. We're the People Behind the Walls."

That reminded Patience of the door into the Keyreeve's office. From the fancy side, it had blended in with the wall, but from her side, it had been a dusty passageway.

She was too distracted to wonder much about that. The crow strutted towards the Fairgate. He held something in his beak.

"And the two kinds of people are different as can be," Reynard went on, "and nothing can change that. It's the way of the world. A place for every person, and every person in her place."

"That hardly seems fair," Patience said, still keeping one eye on the crow.

"Fair? What does that have to do with it?"

"Hrmph."

Reynard stopped pacing. He gave her a sly smile. "But there's one thing, still, to know."

"What's that?" The crow waddled closer. She could see it was a scrap of folded paper in his beak. Scrawls of ink-splotched writing covered the page.

Reynard leaned in very close, right next to her ear. He whispered: "It's all lies."

The crow hopped onto the Fairgate padlock. It winked at her. It jumped through the iron bars. It did not come out the other side.

"Oi!" Patience exclaimed.

Reynard laughed, straightening up. "That's right!" he said. "It's all lies. There aren't two kinds of people. There's only the two places, Out in the Halls and Behind the Walls. And whoever is in one today might easily be in the other one tomorrow."

Patience blinked twice. The crow had indeed vanished into the gate. "How — ?"

"Oh, the worm turns a dozen ways, you can be sure. Why, two hundred years ago, the first Keyreeve was as country-common as you. As for tomorrow, who knows? Maybe his descendant will be out on the street, searching for a place to sweep."

"That's as may be," Patience said, pushing herself up from the curb. "But I should get back to *The Crock and Dice.*"

Leaving Reynard in Fairgate Square, she went home.

Curiosity and determination chased off shame. She didn't care what anyone thought her place should be. Whosebourne was a weird mess from top to bottom, and no one — not fancy in the halls nor plain behind the walls nor who-knows-what from who-knows-where — was going to stop Patience Fell from setting it straight.

But first, she had some answers to get from a woman in an attic room and she meant to get them, even if she had to resort to whacking them loose with a good, stiff broom.

# 18. An Invitation

Patience returned to *The Crock and Dice* too late for supper, but Miss Alys had saved her some stew all the same. The smell of rosemary and sweet, rich roots and thick beef broth banished all questions from her mind. The cook ladled a generous portion into a bowl and set it on the kitchen table.

"Wash up first," she said as Patience went to take a seat.

Patience remembered she was still dirty from squeezing under the Pennywhack fence. She excused herself with a curtsy. While she was scrubbing her face and hands, she decided to change her dress. She wasn't, despite what the Keyreeve said, a complete savage.

"Thank you, ma'am." She took her place at the table.

"Can't have you wasting away," Miss Alys said from the hearth, where she watched for the kettle to boil. "Where would I find another girl with a broom?"

Patience was too preoccupied with dinner to wonder whether that was sarcastic or not.

"So what do you spend your day doing?" Miss Alys asked.

Patience used the time it took to finish a remarkably large mouthful of stew to think of a safe answer. She did *not* want to tell Miss Alys that she'd spent the afternoon at Pennywhack Manor. Too many uncomfortable questions would come of that.

"Oh, I saw a bit of the town," she said. "It's very different than the country."

"That it is." The kettle puffed three times and started to shriek. Miss Alys unhooked it from the spit. She filled the teapot. She set the kettle to the side. "What all did you see?"

"That Fairgate's something, isn't it?"

The cook sniffed. "That rusty old heap? I don't even know why they keep it around."

Fortified by stew, Patience found her curiosity coming back. Between giant bites, she peppered Miss Alys with questions.

"Why is it there? Where is it supposed to go? Did it used to be part of something that went somewhere? Why is there a big lock on it? Are they worried someone will open it so people can go freely from one side of the square to the other which they already do just by walking around it?"

"Gracious!" Miss Alys poured two mugs of tea. "If I could make dinner with questions, we'd feed the town for a week!"

"Well," Patience said in her defense, "it is fox-bonnet odd, isn't it?"

"I suppose."

The cook brought the tea to the table. She set a mug in front of Patience and settled her own bones into a chair with a sigh.

"Everything's odd if you don't know it. But if you're here long enough, you won't even notice any more. It'll all seem right as laundry on a line. You'll think back on the country and wonder how weird it is there compared to here."

"I don't think so." Patience scooped the last spoonful of delicious broth. "But I'm not going anywhere, so I guess we'll see."

"Pfft. That's what they all said."

"The girls before me? Why'd they all leave then?" Patience tried to hide her eagerness to know by intently scraping the bottom of her bowl.

"Hrmph. There's a tale, I suppose." Miss Alys stared into her tea, as if the murky brew held dark secrets. She didn't say more, but looked as though she might. Patience kept as still as she could, waiting for an answer.

A scream from the attic ripped through the inn.

Patience jumped to her feet. Her chair flipped backwards into the pot rack with a great clatter. Miss Alys's tea mug flew into the air. Scalding tea spattered into the fire with a sizzle and burst of steam.

"CROWQUILL!" They cried together.

Grabbing her broom from its place by the door, Patience ran for the attic. Miss Alys followed close behind.

"Everything's fine!" As they tore upstairs, the cook assured the inn customers who'd poked their heads out of doors on every floor. "Quite alright. Fight quine. Everyright allthings."

The attic hatch was shut tight. Thuds and thumps and the whoosh of a strong whirling wind came muffled through the ceiling.

*That's no good,* Patience thought.

"Boost me up," she said to Miss Alys.

"What's in your mind, girl? The hatch's closed as a miser's purse!"

"Just up."

Something WHUMPED right above their heads. The hatch rattled.

"Alright," Miss Alys said. "I hope you've got a good idea."

Patience didn't have a good idea. But she had a pretty good suspicion of who was making all that racket. And she knew what to do about him.

She stepped into the cup of the cook's hands. She pushed herself towards the ceiling. Holding the broom in one hand, she ran her fingers along the hatch crack. Miss Alys wobbled.

"Hold steady!"

"Ooof!"

WHUMP! The hatch rattled again. Patience wedged her pinkie finger in the gap. It pinched terribly, but she could press down and make enough space for her ring finger, then the other two. She pulled the hatch down. Not a moment too soon—Miss Alys' knees gave out and she and Patience and the hatch and ladder all tumbled to the floor.

A snow-storm of Crowquill's papers blizzarded down from the attic.

"She's gone full mad at last!" Miss Alys exclaimed. "Miss Crowquill!" she called up sternly. "That's quite enough of that! We run a respectable establishment!"

Patience leapt to her feet. She seized her broom and charged up the ladder. "It's not her!"

"Daft girl! Don't poke a madwoman with a kitchen broom!"

Patience was already atop the ladder and ready to swing.

Crowquill had wedged herself between her desk and the wall. The offaltosser's whirlwind threw her books and papers every which way. In a calmer moment, Patience might admit the attic mess wasn't *that* different from Crowquill's normal chaos.

The funnel cloud loomed over the cowering poet.

"Oi!" Patience called out. "Remember me?"

The storm spiraled inwards in an instant. The grubby, foul-smelling, wee man stood in its place. He held up his hands. He held out a richly-embossed cream-colored envelope.

"Sorry miss." The offaltosser tugged his forelock. "No harm meant. No need to go brooming."

He struggled with every word. He sweated with the effort of not swearing. "Just delivering the atticmad's invitation."

*Atticmad?*

Patience stepped towards him, brandishing her broom high.

"Flerck!"

He dropped the invitation and, fast as his tiny legs could carry him, sprinted to the window. Patience chased him. She could easily have whacked his rear, but she settled for a near-miss to hurry him on his way. No need for violence. He was, like he said, just delivering the mail.

He jumped to the sill with a mighty leap.

"Be seeing you," he said with a curtsy. Unleashing a torrent of foul words, he spun back into storm-shape and whizzed off into the night.

"Are you alright?" Patience asked Crowquill.

"Y-yes." She stood up. Patience noticed the poet's legs trembled. Crowquill steadied herself against her desk.

Patience picked up the envelope. A red wax blob sealed it shut. The blob bore the impression of a fox's face. "Marquis Goupil."

Miss Alys' head cautiously poked through the hatch. "Girl? Miss Crowquill?"

"Everything i-is fine," Crowquill said. "Just a storm, blew open the windows and startled me."

The cook looked round the wreckage. "A storm, you say."

"It was quite windy," Patience added truthfully. She closed the shutters tight. "That should keep out the night air, ma'am."

Miss Alys squinted at them both. "Now that's all settled. Come Patience, let's leave our guest to her fine mess."

"If you don't mind, ma'am," Patience said, "I could stay and help her clean. I already have my broom."

"It's your day off and time for tea and bed. I can't believe I have to tell a broom-girl this, but there *is* such a thing as working too hard."

"Please?" Crowquill wrung her hands. "It's an awful mess to face alone."

Miss Alys looked for a moment as if she were about to deliver a biting remark about Crowquill and her messes. Instead, she settled for a throaty parting snort.

"Suit yourself. But don't be expecting an easier day tomorrow on account of working late tonight."

"I won't, ma'am." Patience curtsied.

She waited till the cook's footsteps receded to the second floor before turning to face Crowquill. She held up the invitation. Her stern glare could've stripped the stink from an offaltosser.

## 19. A Message from Who-Knows-Where

"I'm not going." Crowquill waved the invitation away. She flumped down onto her bed. "I'm not, I'm not, I'm not."

Patience offered her the offaltosser's envelope again. "You don't even know what it is."

Crowquill turned to face the wall. She clutched her pillow to her chest. Rocking back and forth, she chanted in a tiny sing-song voice:

"Hide away beneath the eaves, stuff the walls with inky sheaves, curl up tight till everyone leaves."

Patience sighed. "You are no help."

The atticmad — for that was what the offaltosser had called her — said nothing in reply.

Patience turned an up-ended chair right-side-up. She sat down. She ran her fingers over the fox face pressed into the red wax seal.

"I'm going to open it."

She waited for Miss Crowquill to object. When she didn't, Patience cracked the wax and fished the invitation out of the envelope. Written in elegant calligraphy, it read:

THE MARQUIS GOUPIL

*Cordially invites you to celebrate the debut presentation of*

*DEMSELLE PATIENCE FELL*

*to the Horned King and Witch Queen*

*upon their triumphant return; and also the Marriage of the Marquis to his beloved*

*THE ATTICMAD PRINCESS CROWQUILL*

*Venue: Fairgate Square*

*Date & Time: One Day Hence, the Witching Hour*

The invitation trembled angrily in Patience's hand when she read her name.

"I don't remember agreeing to be presented anywhere," she growled through gritted teeth. "Especially not at the Witching Hour."

"The Marquis doesn't ask." Crowquill shook her head. "It's beneath him."

"Ah. One of the People in the Fancy Halls, is he?"

"HA!" Crowquill's laugh was harsh and without mirth.

"And what is he to you, Miss Two-Hundred-Years-Old?" Patience whirled on her. "You're going to marry him?"

Crowquill yelped. She plugged her ears. She thunked her head on the wall.

"Pence and pounds, pounds and pence, never make a lick of sense!"

Patience had had all she could stand of the atticmad's rambles. She lunged out of her chair. She grabbed Crowquill by the shoulders.

"Enough!" she cried. "Be useful for once!"

Crowquill covered her face with her feather-filled hair. "Weave my words into an iron fence, madness is the best defense."

Patience shook her. Crowquill just repeated the same phrase 'madness is the best defense' over and over, until Patience pushed her back onto the bed.

"Fine! Just fine!"

She balled her fist and raised it. But she knew she didn't really want to hit Miss Crowquill. She wasn't sure who she wanted to hit. Probably no one deserved it. Except maybe the Keyreeve. But even he couldn't help being the way he was. Like the offaltosser, he was just doing his job.

Patience took five deep breaths and let each one out slowly. When the red spots cleared from her mind, she saw Crowquill was curled up tight on her bed. One black eye glittered from under her mop of wild hair.

*Alright. Time to try something else.*

She'd once watched her father calm a spooked mare. The horse pawed the muddy paddock and lunged at anyone who got too close. She had the same wildness in her eye as Crowquill.

At first, her father just sat on the fence. He'd not paid the mare any attention.

Patience took a step back. She sat down. She stared off at the open hatchway, pretending she was all alone.

Next, her father slowly walked the fence-line round the paddock. He picked up stray bits of hay, making soothing little noises. He acted as though he didn't even know the horse was there. Eventually, the mare stopped pawing the ground and wuffing and carrying on and her father could coax her back into the barn.

Patience got up. She walked over to the hatch. Starting there, she picked up the papers and books and dishes and clothes that were strewn all over the room. She hummed a soothing little tune. She made sure to give Crowquill a lot of space.

It took some doing, but when she was finished, the room was neater than it had probably been in two hundred years.

"There." She put her hands on her hips and surveyed her work. "That's better, isn't it, Miss Crowquill?"

A soft snore was the only reply.

Crowquill had turned her face to the wall and gone to sleep.

*That worked too well. What now?*

She put her hand out to rouse the atticmad, but thought the better of it. Crowquill was so very sound asleep. She reminded Patience of her baby brother, the way he slept with the whole of his body and soul, safe in the knowledge that everything was taken care of.

*Tap... tap... tap...*

The sound on the shutters was soft enough not to disturb the sleeping woman. Patience hefted her broom in one hand, ready to swat the offaltosser if he'd come back. She unlatched the shutters.

A crow waited on the sill. Patience couldn't be sure, but it might have been the same one she had earlier seen fly through the Fairgate and disappear. He had a scrap of paper in his sharp black beak. It was tattered and yellow. It had writing on it. It had been torn from a very old book.

"She's asleep," Patience softly said.

The crow peered round her at the bed. He nodded, then fluttered right at Patience's head!

"Bwah!" she squawked. She slapped her hand over mouth.

The crow landed on her shoulder. The atticmad stirred. She murmured "Johnny?" before settling deeper into her pillow.

Balanced on Patience's shoulder, the crow stretched out his beak. She held out her hand. He dropped the paper into it. He leapt back onto the window sill. He winked.

"Fox in a bonnet." The scrap slipped from her hand.

The bird took to flight, vanishing into the deep dark night.

Patience bent towards the tattered yellow scrap on the floor. She hesitated. She wasn't the sort of person to go through someone else's private mail. On the other hand, Miss Crowquill wouldn't answer any of her questions. And these were extraordinary circumstances. On the other other hand, reading other people's letters without asking was, she knew, as rude as rude got. On the fourth hand…

Quickly, so she wouldn't think herself out of it, she snatched up the page.

It had been torn from another copy of *The Chaos Court* — an entry on the Appletipper. Patience scanned it. Nothing helpful. More interestingly, someone had hand-written a poem in the margins:

*Dearest Love:*

> *The Ending was written right from the Start*
> *Chaos claps in the Beat of your Heart*
> *The Sand scatters round and the Hour grows short*
> *The King and the Queen are coming to Court.*

*I wait for Patience in the Who-Knows-Where,*

*Johnny Factotum*

The midnight wind through the window was warm, but Patience's skin was covered in goosebumps and she shivered from deep down in her belly to the tip-ends of her hair.

## 20. Patience Stays

When Patience got back down to the kitchen, she was surprised to find the lamp still lit. Miss Alys waited at the table, a cold cup of tea at her elbow and a worried purse on her lips. When she saw Patience, the cook sighed.

"I suppose you'll be leaving us, then."

"What?" Patience said. "Why? What did I do?" She thought quick as she could of anything she might have done wrong to be dismissed. "Whatever it was, I'm sorry. Please, I can work harder!"

Now it was the cook's turn to be surprised. "You?" she exclaimed. "You've been nothing but a good broom-girl."

"Then why would you want me to leave?"

"Bless me, I don't! That's the last thing we need, with more guests every season. I just thought — that is — " Miss Alys nudged a stool out from under the table. "Have a seat."

Putting her broom in its place on the wall, Patience came over and took her place on the stool. Miss Alys looked her straight in the eye. She furrowed her brow. The low hiss and pop of the dying fire filled the long, silent moment before she spoke.

"I've been sitting here in the dead of night, instead of in bed, which is where my bones want nothing but to be. Why?"

Patience could tell it wasn't the kind of question that wanted answering, so she said nothing.

"I've been waiting on you to come down and announce you've had enough of all these strange town doings and are leaving us for good. Just like every broom-girl we've had, once — " her voice got hushed, " — once they take up with Miss Crowquill."

Patience shifted on her stool. She remembered how, not too many nights ago, she had packed her things into a bindle and almost done that exact thing — without even the courtesy of a good-bye or note.

"Things might be strange here, to me," she said, "but someone told me strange is only strange till you forget it's not what you've always known."

"She's a wise woman who said it, but things in this inn *are* strange and no amount of forgetting is going to make that change."

Crowquill's invitation and the poem scrap felt very big in Patience's apron pocket just then. "You said the other girls left. What happened to them?"

"Hrmph. To hear them tell it, you'd think the end of the world paid them a personal visit."

Patience didn't trust herself to say anything. She wondered if any of the previous broom girls had seen invitations with their names on them.

"They'd talk of cursing storms and dancing goats and all manner of whatnot I've never seen nor heard of," Miss Alys continued. "And, after a while, every one of them got wild round the eyes when it was their turn to take Miss Crowquill her breakfast."

She leaned forward. "Except for you." She jabbed one gnarled, mottled finger at her. "You jump right up into the madwoman's nest, without so much as a flinch. And then you come back, hours later, brushing your hands from a job well done."

"It's my place," Patience mumbled.

"Eh?"

She repeated herself. Miss Alys snorted.

"It was their place too, the other gaggle of weeping ninnies who fled my kitchen, skirting and squeaking at every stray bit of windblown trash."

Patience hesitated before asking her next question. But she had to know.

"Begging your pardon, ma'am, but why haven't you sorted it out? It being your place too?"

"And when am I supposed to do that? I'm run near off my feet all day, keeping up with the plain ordinaries of this world."

"Sorry, I just thought—"

Miss Alys wasn't done. "One broom-girl leaves, I've got a big empty hole of work to fill. A new one shows up and there's only me to train her up to do that work. By the time she's worth anything, she's in the wind and I'm back where I started."

She shook one crooked finger. "Don't be asking me to sort it out. I've got enough trouble to spare keeping the grumble-bellies out there from wrecking the place three times a day. And that's even if I knew what was going on. Which I don't."

The cook settled back in her chair. She watched the fire ebb. When she spoke again, it was soft, almost to herself.

"But you. There's something different about you. That something might be good and it might be bad, but whatever it is, it makes you face right at the strange and dangerous and, chin-up, say 'I'll stay.'"

Patience stared at the hearth. She knew questions were coming. Questions she wasn't sure how to answer, not without being trundled off to a madhouse or being whipped and jailed by the Keyreeve's men.

"I don't know why I'm like that," she said. "It's my... I'm just... Someone has to..."

She tried hard to herd her words together, but her mind was tired and overfull; her thoughts escaped like a flock of sheep in a thick, damp fog.

Just then, the midnight bell tolled from the town's clock tower. *Thwong… thwong… thwong…*

With every stroke, her eyelids drooped and her head tipped forward onto her chest. *Thwong… thwong… thwong…* She struggled hard against the pull of the looming dark. *Thwong… thwong… thwong…* She drifted into the warm sea of sleep, lifted up and carried into nothing… *Thwong… thwong… thwong…*

On the last stroke of the bell, Miss Alys set her down in her bed. The cook pulled the covers up to Patience's chin and tucked her in.

"Hush," Miss Alys whispered, "it's the Witching Hour now. Long past time for a brave girl to be abed. You stay, and we'll sort out tomorrow's trouble tomorrow."

Patience heard her blow out the lamp with a little puff.

The dark got even darker.

## 21. A Thoughtful Picnic in Fairgate Square

Patience lay curled up in bed, content as a barn cat in a patch of sun. Sleep wrapt her round and she snuggled into its warm forgetful folds. Sounds and smells drifted through the half-open door; conversations and pan-clatters, meat and potatoes. Somewhere far away, a muffled bell rang. She had no idea what that meant. Only on the twelfth stroke did she wake up enough to remember. She had duties to attend to!

"Noon!" She leapt to her feet. "Noon! Noon noon noon! No no no!"

Sleep-creased and rumpled, she ran to the kitchen.

"Sorry, sorry, sorry!" She snatched an apron off a hook. She tied it round her waist, forgetting that she still had on her apron from yesterday.

"What are you sorrying on about, girl?"

Miss Alys turned a roast on the spit with one hand while pulling a rack of bread from the oven with the other. She spun round, leaving the spit to go on its own momentum for a turn or two. Shaking the loaves onto three plates, she scooped up five mugs in her free hand. She stepped lightly cross the kitchen floor, flipped the ale tap with the edge of the bread rack, and filled the mugs without spilling a drop. It was a ballet worthy of a gabledancer.

"Let me help!" Patience was mortified at having slept so late. She seized the spit and cranked the roast at a furious pace.

"Oh no you don't!" Miss Alys dropped the rack. She swatted Patience away with the pot holder. "One day off every fortnight, that's your right. I won't have anyone saying I treat my girls unfair."

"But yesterd—"

"But what?" With several deft strokes, Miss Alys sliced meat onto each of the three bread plates. "I remember it you worked yesterday. Cleaning up after Miss Crowquill. That means you're overdue for a free day."

Patience stared at her, confused.

"If you want to spend your precious time sleeping," the cook continued, "or gawking at me while I work for two, that's your business."

"But—"

" — if it were me I'd want to get out and about. Maybe see what strange and dangerous doings are afoot in old Whosebourne town."

Finally, Patience took the hint. She let go of the spit and curtsied. "Thank you, ma'am."

"There's a lunch packed," Miss Alys shouted over her shoulder as she bustled out to the common room.

Patience spied a lumpy burlap sack on the table by the door. Taking off the extra apron, she grabbed the sack and went back out on the town.

There was no question where to go first. Somehow — though she still didn't know how — the Fairgate was the center of all this mess. If she was going to sort it out and clean it up, that was the place to start.

As always, Fairgate Square stood empty. Patience marched right up to the iron monument. Dropping the lunch sack, she shook the bars. They rattled in a satisfying way. She tugged on the padlock. It did not open. She took a deep breath and stuck her hand through the gate.

Fingers came out the other side. They looked like her fingers. They were connected to her hand, just like always. She wiggled them to make sure. They wiggled back.

"Hrmph."

She knew she'd seen a crow fly through the bars and disappear.

*The gate goes somewhere. At the same time, it doesn't.*

The thought affronted her. That wasn't how things worked — or at least, it wasn't how things were supposed to work.

"I don't like it."

The empty square didn't seem to care.

Patience sat on the stone ground. She leaned back against the gate. She rummaged lunch out of the sack. As she did, something crumpled in her apron pocket. She took out the Marquis' invitation to Crowquill and the torn page from *The Chaos Court* with the creepy poem. She set them on the ground, side by side. Gnawing a hunk of dark rye bread, she read them both over several times.

## THE MARQUIS GOUPIL

*Cordially invites you to celebrate the debut presentation of*

### DEMSELLE PATIENCE FELL

*to the Horned King and Witch Queen*

*upon their triumphant return; and also the Marriage of the Marquis to his beloved*

### THE ATTICMAD PRINCESS CROWQUILL

*Venue: Fairgate Square*

*Date & Time: One Day Hence, the Witching Hour*

*Dearest Love:*

> *The Ending was written right from the Start*
> *Chaos claps in the Beat of your Heart*
> *The Sand scatters round and the Hour grows short*
> *The King and the Queen are coming to Court.*

> *I wait for Patience in the Who-Knows-Where,*

> *Johnny Factotum*

"The Ending was written right from the Start…"

*That hardly leaves any point in doing anything. So that can't be true.*

She kept on puzzling.

"Chaos claps in the Beat of your Heart… the King and the Queen are coming to Court."

*That's the Chaos Court, that's clear. Clear as a lump of coughed-up cud. Bluh.*

*Wait!*

The Marquis' invitation wasn't just to present Patience to the King and Queen. He was also going to marry 'The Atticmad Princess Crowquill.'

"And she seemed right happy about that." Patience snorted. "About as happy as a sheep about to be sheared with a wolf's teeth."

'Princess' Crowquill meant that she was the King and Queen's daughter. Why they were who-knows-where and Crowquill was stuck in the attic of *The Crock and Dice*,

Patience couldn't figure. She thought royalty kept its own kin close by.

The King and Queen (and the rest of their mad Court) must be somewhere they could not easily get to Whosebourne from. Judging by the picture of all the wild creatures at the front of Johnny Factotum's book, it would take more than a thousand country miles to keep them from a good rampage.

*Factotum…*

He'd written the book on the Chaos Court—the only book the Keyreeve ever bothered to read. A book of secrets no one was supposed to know. The same Factotum who signed the crow-brought poem? He had to be.

Not two days ago, Patience would've figured he wrote it two hundred years ago, back around the time of his great big book.

Now though… now she couldn't take anything for granted. Johnny Factotum might be long dead, he might be two hundred years old, he might be a thousand. He might be a normal man. He might be a pile of books that liked throwing other books around.

*Whoever he is, he's the one Crowquill really loves. At least, if the way she keeps saying 'my Johnny' means anything. And he called her his 'Dearest Love'. So it goes both ways.*

Patience didn't know much about people in love. But if all the stories had any truth to them, it was harder to keep two lovers apart than it was to keep a King and Queen from their Princess—or a mother and father from their daughter if she needed help.

*So he's somewhere unreachable too. And waiting for me, by the note.*

She washed down the bread with a long drink from a jug of water Miss Alys had packed. She felt the Fairgate, cold and hard, against her back. She thought of the crow, who somehow knew how to fly in one side and not out the other, bringing scraps of paper back and forth.

*Waiting in the Who-Knows-Where...*

It had been a productive thoughtful lunch. She didn't have any answers. But she'd winnowed down the questions to a manageable few. Time to do something about them.

She set the last crust of bread by the Fairgate for a future crow. "I just hope that hole is still under the fence."

## 22. A Convenient Ladder

Patience walked past Pennywhack Manor, fast as she could without looking like she was hiding something. She had decided it would be easier to sneak in after nightfall, but she wanted to make sure the burrow under the hedges was still there.

"That's luck," she said to herself when she spotted the edge of the hole hidden beneath the thick branches. "Reynard must not've said anything."

Keeping her head down, she strode briskly onward.

Movement caught her eye as she passed a break in the hedges. She glanced over. The sight stopped her in her tracks.

Linus, dressed up in a tight, bright red uniform, marched up and down a wide green field. On one side of the pitch, the Keyreeve perched on an elevated chair, like a dairy cow on a fence post. He held an enormous conical megaphone in front of his face, into which he barked:

"Hup-HO, hup-HO, hup-HO!"

"Oh. You poor boy," Patience whispered.

"Bout-FAY!" the Keyreeve bellowed as his nephew reached the edge of the grass.

Even from the fence, Patience could hear Linus wheeze. His face was almost as red as the uniform and it glowed like the brass buttons in the pitiless afternoon sun.

"Doub-Tie-YUM!"

Her friend struggled to speed up. It hurt her to watch him work so hard and cover so little ground.

"Huphohuphohuphohuphohuphho!" the Keyreeve shouted so fast, he lost his own breath. He lowered the megaphone, coughing. He waved one hand and a servant handed him up a glass of water. He waved again and another servant exchanged the megaphone for a wide feather fan, which the Keyreeve worked furiously to cool himself.

Linus seized the opportunity to rest. He bent over, but the uniform was so stiff he only made it halfway. His uncle gasped something Patience couldn't hear. He jabbed a thick finger toward the boy.

One of the servants—she thought it might be Reynard—sauntered out onto the marching pitch. When he got there, he whispered in Linus' ear. He pointed to the ground.

Linus shook his head. Reynard pointed again. Linus dropped down and began doing push-ups. He made it to seven before collapsing face-first into the grass.

Reynard put a hand on his shoulder. From her vantage point, Patience could see he had smuggled out a canteen. He gave Linus a few surreptitious sips, shielding him from the Keyreeve's sight with his body.

"Huurrrup!"

With a great big wheeze, the boy pushed himself to standing. His uncle resumed shouting cadence and Linus marched on.

"Stay strong," Patience said, though she knew he couldn't hear. "I'll spring you soon as it's dark."

Regretfully leaving her friend to suffer, she retreated to plan his rescue.

By the time the ninth bell's toll rolled over the town, Patience had her plan figured out. She crept from the alley where she'd been skulking. She double-timed back to Pennywhack Manor. All along the way, her head swiveled at every sound, but none of the Fair Folk were around.

She wriggled under the Manor fence. She didn't care how muddy it made her. If she got caught, the Keyreeve's contempt would be the least of her problems. And Linus didn't seem to mind.

Flattening herself against the abandoned garden shed, she peeked round the corner. The path towards the main house wasn't lit here, but lamps glowed all round the mansion.

"Now," she muttered, "where's your room, Linus Pennywhack?"

She wished she'd paid more attention the last time she'd been there. But how could she have known she'd need to sneak into the house like a fox into a pantry?

She pushed the wish away. She had plans. Plans were better than wishes.

On the very edge of lamp-light, she crept through the moon-shadows. She could see a guard at the gate, his back to her, but no one else was out and about. She made her way round to the back of the mansion. She reasoned that any little doors for the People Behind the Walls would be there, out of sight of the People in the Fancy Halls.

If that didn't work she could always try the Widow's Walk again.

The moment she stepped round the corner, she spotted something better than a servants' entrance. A telescope glinted in a half-open window on the second floor. Moonlight winked from the lens, as if signaling a friendly 'up here, up here!'

Linus' bedroom, though, was dark. Patience bent down and picked up a pebble. She tossed it underhand. It tapped on the sill. No lights went on. She tried another rock, a bit harder. Still nothing. If she threw any harder, she'd break the glass.

"Hsst!"

There was no reply. She daren't make any more noise than that.

*He must be asleep. Wore out from all that marching.*

She snuck directly under the window. She meant to find a drain pipe to shimmy up. It'd be like climbing a tree, she reckoned. But things were really going her way, because somebody'd left a ladder in the ivy right under Linus' bedroom.

Hoisting it up felt like wrestling a ram into the shearing pen—a very long ram who wasn't about to go gentle to the sheep-barber. The ladder almost fell backwards, then lunged sideways. She yanked it back, overcorrected, and it nearly hit the ground. She heaved it up. It waved dangerously round. With a mighty pull, she managed to not put it through a window. Finally, she wrangled it into place. It hit Linus' sill with a *THUNK!*

She dove into the bushes. She held very, very still, ears pricked and quivering. The night-time town sounds were all she could hear—that and the thunderous *THWUB THWUB THWUB* of her heart.

She had to move. She wanted to wait more to be *sure* sure no one heard the kerfluffle she'd made. But the longer she waited, the more likely it was someone would stroll by or glance out a window and spot the ladder. Taking a great big gulp, she jumped to her feet. Quick as a squirrel after the last fall nut, she scampered up to Linus' room.

*Whonnnkk… sneeeee… whonnnkk… sneeee…*

She stifled a giggle at Linus' extraordinary snore. Pitch dark as the room was, she could find him easy enough. She moved slowly toward the sound, remembering the tables filled with pots and tubes and glass-topped cases. She held her hands in front of her as she went.

The tables had been taken away.

*Probably the Keyreeve's punishment.*

By rights, she felt, the pompous wigged wobbler ought to be marched back and forth 'cross a sunny field till he learned a thing or two about respecting people's property.

Her shin bumped Linus' bed. She fumbled the covers till she held what felt like a shoulder.

"Oi," she whispered, shaking him. "Wakey wake."

"Mrphl." He rolled over. "Ten more minutes, Mother."

*He must be back home in his dreams.*

Patience was reluctant to wake him from pleasant memories, but she needed his help. And he needed hers. And there wasn't much time for either of them. She shook him harder.

He burrowed into the bed. "Frrf mrbts, Mrfr."

Time for the direct approach. She felt round for his nose. She pinched it shut. After a moment, he sat bolt upright gasping.

"Whuh! Sir, yes, sir! Awake and reporting, sir!"

She let go of his nose. She put a finger over his lips. "Shhh. It's me."

"Miss Fell? What are you —"

"—I'm here to rescue you."

"Rescue? What are you talking about? Hold on."

He rustled around. *Scritch... scritch... pop!* A match flared to light. He touched it to the wick of a bedside lamp and blew it out. Putting on his glasses, he squinted at her.

"It *is* you! That's very nice."

The way he said it made her smile in spite of herself.

His eyes widened. "But you can't be here! My uncle promised to have you whipped and imprisoned if you came back!"

"Pfft to that!" She punched him on the shoulder. "Come on. There's a ladder someone left lying around. We have to hurry down before they come back for it."

"I can't."

"Why not? Of course you can. Are you sore and wore out from all that marching? Just climb down slow. I'll be there every rung of the way."

"It's not that."

"Then why?"

He smoothed out his blanket. He looked round at the bare bookshelves and tables. He sighed. "This is my place in the world. I may not like it much right now, but it's my place."

Patience understood.

She understood, but she did not accept it.

She knew from the set, stubborn expression on Linus' face that there would be no budging him to escape—at least not by arguing. She'd climb that ladder when they came to it.

"If you're not going to take my help, there's a second reason I came. I need your help."

"That, I can do. As long as it doesn't entail escape."

*We'll see about that, clever boy.*

"Of course not."

Hastily, she sketched out what she had learned about Johnny Factotum, the Fair Folk, and the Chaos Court. She described the crow hopping to nowhere through the Fairgate. She told him about the reappearance of the offaltosser. She showed him Crowquill's invitation. As the capstone, she gave him Factotum's strange snippet of poetry about the King and Queen coming to court.

As she talked, Linus' breath quickened. He leaned forward with an intense stare, all traces of sleep gone.

"The King and Queen are coming to town? Can you imagine if everything we saw in the front of the book showed up in Whosebourne all at once?"

Patience pictured the wreckage. "It would be very, very bad."

"I don't think anyone can say it's not my place to stop it." He swung his legs round as if he might leap up at any moment to run down the truth like a hound. "The Marquis is the key to the whole thing. We need that book to look him up. And we need to not get caught retrieving it from my uncle's office."

"I have a plan."

"I'd expect nothing less."

How he flustered her with his compliments!

## 23. Behind the Walls

The Keyreeve had locked Linus' door from the outside. That suited Patience just fine. He would figure no one could get in or out. But she didn't plan on taking the door just anyone could see.

While Linus ducked behind a screen to get dressed, she picked up the lamp and closely scanned the walls. She ignored the wall to the outside and the wall to the Fancy Halls. There wouldn't be anything hidden there.

By the time Linus emerged, crookedly tucking in his shirt, she'd found it. A thin crack ran from the floor to about three hands over her head. It turned a right angle and vanished behind one of the empty bookcases.

"Help me move this."

Without question, he took up his post on one side of the shelves. She bent her knees and grabbed the other side. The bookcase was quite heavy. They had to rock it back and forth to wiggle it out of their way. This was not made any easier by the need to be very quiet.

When they'd managed to slide it just far enough from the wall to squeeze behind it, Patience reached around. She felt under the chair railing for a latch. She hadn't seen Reynard open the hidden door to the Keyreeve's office, but she reasoned there had to be a latch on the Fancy side. Otherwise servants would get themselves stuck on the wrong side of the wall.

Her fingers found a switch hidden in a niche under the railing. She flipped it.

"There we go!"

The wall detached and swung inwards, revealing a dim, narrow hallway.

"I say," Linus whispered. "That's brilliant. How did you know that was there?"

"It's a servant door."

"I don't follow."

She just waited, till he figured it out.

"Oh! Right. Of course. I forget you're a—well, that is, you're so clever and confident and not obedient." He flushed. "Not that I mean—oh bother. No offense intended."

"You watch yourself, Master Pennywhack." She gave him a fake-stern glare that turned into a grin. She hooked the lamp and swung it towards the dark entry. "Come on. Squeeze through."

"After you, Miss Fell."

Once behind the walls, Patience paused to figure out where to go. She tried to picture the whole massive mansion in her head. She was almost sure the Keyreeve's office was on the third floor. But it could have been the fourth. Linus kept talking, which didn't help her concentrate one bit.

"I can't believe all this is back here. I had no idea. I wonder how extensive these passages are? And if you can get from—OH!" He smacked his forehead.

Patience jumped. "What?!"

"I just figured it out. Well, not *it*. But an it. Part of it, maybe. Maybe not figured it out. But I have a hypothesis."

"A what? What are you jibberjabbing about now?"

She didn't mean to snap, but she was trying to work out directions in her head in a place where she'd never been and that was taking all her extra thought, leaving none to spare for being nice.

"A hypothesis. It's an idea—a guess about how things might be that you can test by investigating. But I digress. What I think I've figured out is—"

"Talk while we walk," Patience said, leading the way. "Quietly, in case someone is delivering a late night snack."

"Of course." He continued in a somewhat theatrical whisper. "I suspect I know where the Fair Folk come from. Where the Chaos Court is—the ones who aren't here, anyway."

"Where?"

"From behind the Fairgate."

"Impossible. Behind the Fairgate there's just more square."

"So it would seem. But these secret servant halls made me think. And the bird you saw go through without coming out the other side. What if there's a place that's behind the walls of the world?"

"Like a 'Who-Knows-Where'?"

"Exactly. Just like where Johnny Factotum said he was in the note."

"Waiting for me."

"That may not be quite the case." He chuckled as if he'd made a joke. "Case."

They reached an intersection. After a brief hesitation, Patience pointed.

"This way." She was guessing, but she didn't want to worry him, so she led with confidence.

"Case, you see," he persisted. "You may have noticed that Johnny Factotum writes in the old style."

"A bit." She remembered how challenging the pieces of *The Chaos Court* she'd read were. Very, very old style.

"Back then, the convention was to use uppercase for all nouns. Do you know why it's called uppercase?"

She didn't answer. They stood at a spiral staircase. "Wait here."

Doing her best to act like she belonged, she hurried up the stairs as if on an errand. No one waited at the top.

"Whist," she called down and waved Linus up.

"It's because printers keep the capital letters for the press in cases on top of the cases with the small letters. Uppercase, see?"

"What in the mad March wood does this have to do with anything?" She couldn't help but sound like her mother, fed up with childish prattle.

"I was merely observing that when Factotum wrote 'Patience' he might not have been talking about you. He could have just been talking about the cardinal virtue."

*You daft chattering boy...*

Patience didn't want to fight with him, so she bit back her words and concentrated on finding the servant-side of the Keyreeve's door.

"Regardless of what he meant, it's more than likely that Johnny Factotum is locked away behind the Fairgate too. I don't know how any of this is possible or why it has to be kept a big secret, though. I'm hoping that perhaps a focused perusal of the book my uncle purloined will elucidate—"

Just then, Patience saw a black bushy tail, hanging round the corner in the shadows up ahead.

"Aha!"

She sprinted towards the Marquis.

It wasn't him. A careless servant had dropped a furniture-duster there and left it, drooped like a fox tail on the floor.

Linus ambled up to her. He moved as though he were much too sore to be running anywhere.

"What was that all about?"

Patience couldn't believe her luck. The duster lay right in front of a door. And on the door was a tarnished brass plaque that read *K.Rv. Off.* She'd stumbled into exactly the right spot.

"Tumbled off the barn into a pile of goosedown pillows," she murmured.

"Eh?"

"Never mind. We're here."

## 24. Hidden in Plain Sight

Patience cracked the office door. No light came through. But maybe someone was hiding in the dark. In a fake voice as fancy as she could muster, she called out:

"Sir, late night tea, sir."

No reply. She still didn't trust the Keyreeve didn't lurk, waiting to pounce. Then she had an image of the enormous official crouched behind his desk, sticking out on both ends. She was being silly. She snorted and went into the office.

"I suspect the book is in his desk." Linus moved round her. "He seemed very keen on taking that specific book. He ordered the rest of them returned to the attic. But that one —" He stopped behind the desk. "Do you think he really knows about the Chaos Court and is hiding it?"

Patience didn't want to speak ill of a friend's relative (not even the Keyreeve), so she shrugged.

"No sense chasing five hens at once."

"Hens? You do have an odd way of putting things."

"One question at a time."

"Yes, of course." He pursed his lips. He rummaged through the desk's drawers.

The moment he'd asked if the Keyreeve knew about the Chaos Court, Patience knew the answer had to be 'Yes!' If Linus' uncle had really thought the offaltosser was just silly country superstition, he wouldn't have bothered squelching a broom-girl who worked at a common inn. But what did he know and when did he know it?

"Here we go!" Linus pulled Crowquill's leek-stained book out of the desk. He squinted in the drawer. "There are four more copies of the same book."

*Makes sense*, Patience thought, but did not say. *If he wanted to keep it quiet, hide all the copies of the book he never allowed printed in the first place.*

Linus sat. He opened the book to the front and then back. "Of course. No table of contents or index. Where to begin?"

"M for Marquis?"

He had already begun riffling through the book. "M... ma... mar... nothing. Hrm. What if..."

Pages fluttered back and forth as he jumped around *The Chaos Court*. He muttered to himself, just like when he'd been working at his board. He jotted notes in a curly scribble script.

There wasn't anything she could think of to do to help. She put the lamp next to him on the table and paced round the large room. The lamp was scarcely necessary, as bright moonlight flooded in through the floor-to-ceiling windows. She could make out every detail of the paintings that crowded the walls.

The pictures were all different, but also all the same. There was always one important person in the middle of the scene, wearing the fanciest clothes. The important people all looked like Linus. They were in the middle of doing something—hunting on horseback or judging a cow at a contest or writing in a book with a big feather pen while gazing off into the distance at something very serious.

Every one of them had a key hung round their necks.

Patience glanced over at the one glass display case in the room. The snow-white cushion inside gleamed in the moonlight. At its center, black as night, nestled a common iron key.

*A symbol of my office, brubarubaruba*, the Keyreeve had said.

"This is interesting," Linus called out without looking up from the book. "Factotum writes: 'the touch of iron is most loathsome to the Fair Folk and causes them great pain.' That explains why they can't just open the Fairgate. And perhaps why the Fairgate was built to begin with."

"It explains a lot."

She returned to the paintings. The various Keyreeves weren't the only people in them. All round the pleasant man judging the cow, a crowd of farmers waited for the results. Their excited faces wouldn't have been out of place back home. One other fellow in the scene wasn't country though. Just behind the Keyreeve, a man in a red coat held a silver platter with green, yellow, and blue ribbons. His nose wrinkled at the cow.

Something about him was familiar.

Patience moved on to the next painting.

A hunting Keyreeve pointed onward from atop a rearing horse. Behind him, several boys held baying dogs on leashes. Next to the horse, a bored man in a red coat handed the rider his hunting rifle.

It was the same man as in the cow-judging. In the tricky moonlight though, it was hard to figure out why she felt she knew him.

"Ah! Now we're getting somewhere," she heard Linus say behind her. "The Goupil, self-styled Marquis by his own clever design..."

Patience barely listened. She moved from picture to picture, ignoring all the other figures except that man in the red coat. He appeared again and again, always at the Keyreeve's side. She followed him back through history, to the oldest painting in the room.

A brass plaque on the frame read: ALDO PENNYWHACK SAVES WHOSEBOURNE.

The artist had captured Aldo in the middle of locking the Fairgate as a host of townsfolk cheered him on. Not everyone was cheering. Hidden amid the happy crowd, the man in the red coat lurked. His lip curled a nasty snarl, showing sharp bright teeth.

"Will shift his shape from fox to man and back again." Linus stopped reading. "Patience! The Marquis! The Marquis Goupil is—"

But Patience already knew. "He's Reynard. And he wants us to steal the Town Key."

"Very clever, Demselle Fell," the fox purred from the secret doorway. "You didn't even need Factotum's silly book to figure it out."

## 25. The Key

"Two hundred years." The Marquis strode forward. Between steps, the fox shapeshifted into Reynard. "I've wasted two centuries among you dullards, waiting for someone clever enough to solve my little riddles and brave enough to do what needs to be done."

Linus rose to his feet. "How did you stay in my family's employ for so long without anyone realizing you were the same person over and over?"

"Who would realize? None of you bother to notice servants. Isn't that right, Miss Fell?"

Patience knew what he was talking about. "'The better you do your job,'" she quoted Miss Alys from her first day in town, "'the less anyone should know you're there.'"

Linus frowned. "Be that as it may, I find it implausible that—"

"Oh shut up," Reynard said.

"Brub," was all Linus could manage in his shock.

"That's better. Now, if you will, Demselle Fell, you know what I want."

"I'm not stealing the key so you can open up the Fairgate and let all those creatures out."

The Marquis chuckled. "Yes. You will. Your obstinance makes you ideal for my purposes, but I expected it would also be a sticking point."

He clapped his hands.

Shivtickle squeezed through the servant door. The jamb cracked a little as his shoulders forced their way. His head brushed the flying babies painting on the ceiling. Coinquaff toddled in after him. He blocked the doorway, swaying on his heels. The Marquis surveyed his minions.

"Ah, there's the night shift. The boy, if you would."

The thugs marched over to Linus. He hugged the book to his chest. He cried out with pain when they seized his arms and hoisted him out of the chair.

Patience ran to the window. She threw it open. She could see a guard at the gate and a servant wandering the grounds. She took a deep breath.

"By all means," Reynard-Goupil said. "Call for help. I'm certain the Keyreeve will be happy to know there is an intruder in his house."

Patience wished she had a broom to whack the smug off his face.

"And of course, there's the matter of your friend." He nodded at Coinquaff and Shivtickle. They lifted Linus off the ground. They swung him once towards the open window and set him back down hard.

Patience closed the window.

"Does my uncle know what you're up to?!" Linus' face was bright red.

"That towering pile of pudding? He doesn't even know what I'm up to when I'm up to something legitimate."

Cruel rage flashed in the fox-man's eyes. "It's obscene. I, of noble blood — of the noblest blood — who by rights should be King-in-Waiting of the Chaos Court, am forced to serve that clod of greasy common clay, that son of a son of a street-boy."

"You should be proud. It's your place in the world." Patience hoped to goad him into shouting at her. Maybe someone would hear. Even if she got whipped, at least he'd be exposed and Linus would be safe from being tossed out the window.

The Marquis was too refined for that. He just smiled a polite smile, with a hint of teeth under his upper lip. "The only place, Demselle Fell, is the one we take."

He looked her right in the eyes. She did not like what she saw.

"And it's time for me to take what's mine. With your kind help, of course."

"She'll never help you!" Linus shouted.

"Do be kind." Reynard-Goupil waved one finger. His gaze never left Patience. Shivtickle clapped his hand over Linus' nose and mouth, cutting off his air.

"He's right," Patience said. "Whatever you want, I'm sure it's bad and I won't help."

The Marquis walked over to the display case with the Fairgate key. "You Plain Folk." He rested his fingers on the edge of the case. "You are so bad at foretelling the future."

With a sudden blow of his elbow, he shattered the glass.

"Now," he said, brushing shards of glass from his red coat, "before your friend suffocates, I suggest you pick up that key."

Linus fought as hard as he could to get free. He might as well have tried to lift the whole of Pennywhack Manor. Shivtickle kept on smothering him, not even flexing a muscle.

Patience walked over next to the Marquis. The Fairkey nestled black on the white silk pillow. *The touch of iron...* she remembered Linus reading, *causes them great pain.*

"No, I cannot touch it," the Marquis said, as if reading her mind. "For two hundred years my victory has lain right there as I waited for just the right person to pick it up for me."

"I've never stolen anything."

"Of course you have. You live in a stolen town, built on power stolen from *my* crown. Your whole place in this world is nothing but one enormous insolent crime."

Behind her, Linus' muffled cries grew weaker. The key's sharp iron teeth glittered in the moonlight.

"Yes," the Marquis acknowledged. "You *could* use that blasted metal against me. But could you hit all three of us? Not in time. Your friend would die. You have no choice, broom-girl. You are powerless, I am powerful, and each of us is in our place."

"For now." She picked up the Fairkey. She clenched it so hard in her fist that it cut her. *For now.*

The Marquis snapped his fingers. Shivtickle let Linus' face go. He gasped great gulps of air. His face slowly turned from purple to its normal color.

"Well done, Demselle Fell." He gestured to the thugs. They heaved Linus up and man-handled him through the servants' door.

"What now?" Patience asked when they were alone.

The town bell tolled nearby. Twelve loud tones rolled over Pennywhack Manor.

"The Witching Hour."

Patience remembered the invitation. "My debut presentation."

"And my long-awaited wedding. The pieces are set and they all tumble down." Reynard-Goupil turned back into a fox. "The Chaos Court is coming to town."

## 26. A Walk at the Witching Hour

The streets were empty. Patience thought back to her first day in town. All those people. More people than she'd even known there were in the world, all jostling her every which way. But now, not even one late-night walker was out to raise the alarm.

Ten paces ahead of her, Coinquaff and Shivtickle frog-marched Linus towards Fairgate Square. The Marquis trotted along beside her. His nose stuck in the air as though he hadn't a care. She supposed he hadn't, thanks to her.

"Why so quiet, Demselle?" he asked after a few blocks. "I do hope you are not too downcast at being so well-tricked."

She didn't trust herself to answer without offaltosser words.

"Think of it this way: if it were not for your true quality, however common, you wouldn't have been able to serve my plot so well."

"Oh. I guess that makes it all better."

The Marquis ignored her sarcasm. "It's an honor, really. A testament to your excellence. In all this time, no one has been brave or clever or resourceful enough to get anywhere near the Fairkey, let alone steal it. And that is not for lack of trying on my part. But a craftsman is only as good as his tools, and those who came before you..." He gave a dismissive wave of his paw. "Frail work-things all."

"The other broom-girls." That mystery at least had been solved. "You tried to get them to learn about the Chaos Court and they ran away."

"Not just broom-girls! Stable boys, garden gaffers, and more washerwomen than stones in a cobblemauler's shoe."

"But not me."

"Not you! You are magnificent. Persistent and smart. Why, I'd wager a week of Coinquaff's wages you probably wouldn't even have needed the ladder I left you to get to Linus' room."

Patience couldn't tell whether his praise was real or he was making fun of her. She didn't know which would have made her stomach hurt worse.

"And you're the one who told the Keyreeve I'd seen the offaltosser."

"Guilty. It was the best way to get you into his office for the first time, so you could see the key. Plant the seed, as it were, for the future theft."

"And if I did come back, he'd punish me if I got caught. So I'd have to be sneaky about it, which meant I couldn't get help when you showed up."

The fox skipped a step in surprise. "Very good! For a Plainfolk girl, your mind is almost devious enough to be Fair."

"And Crowquill?" Patience wasn't sure why the villain was being so forthcoming with his plots, nor what she could do with the information at this late hour. But she figured knowing more was better than knowing less, if she ever got the chance for revenge.

"What of her?"

"Was that all a show too? The shoe? Is she really on your side?"

"She will be."

"What does that mean? It seems like she played your plan perfect. If it hadn't been for her showing me Factotum's book—"

"A silly book!" The Marquis snapped sharp teeth at the night air. "Written by a nobody! Slander and lies, where it isn't nonsense!"

She'd struck a nerve. She jabbed again. "Miss Crowquill thinks highly of it. She's always on about her dear Johnny. You say you want to marry her, but I think she loves—"

"Princess Crowquill doesn't know what is good for her. And neither, if you continue yammering, do you."

As long as Linus was in the grip of the Marquis' thugs, Patience was reluctant to push the fox further. They walked on in silence for two blocks. No one appeared to rescue her. She and Linus were on their own.

"Why not have one of your cruel men nick the key?" she asked, pointing at Coinquaff and Shivtickle.

"Shivtickle?" the Marquis called out. "Show her how you got your name."

The brute lifted up one enormous hand. He flexed his fingers. They turned into long, sharp, thin knife blades. He wiggled them at her. With a flick of his wrist, they were fingers again.

"We would need a tavern to properly show off Coinquaff's gifts, but I think you get the picture."

"Yes." *They're Fair Folk just like you. That means iron will hurt them too.*

"And, before you ask, I couldn't use any of the Pennywhack servants either. They are Plain as clay, but they do need their jobs and won't risk them for petty theft." The Marquis had gotten over his fit of pique and was talking in his fancy, generous fashion again.

"No," he continued with a lordly wave of his paw, "I needed someone no one would expect. Someone who could work behind the walls, but who didn't mind stepping out of her place when she needed to. Someone, in short, like you."

Patience felt as though, for all the talking the fox was doing, there was a great deal he wasn't saying. She probed more. "It seems complicated, waiting for just the right person for the job."

"You've no idea."

"But why not just get the Keyreeve himself to do whatever it is you needed? I'm sure you could fool him into it, you being so clever."

"Ah, were it so simple." The Marquis sighed. "He'd never go along, no matter how good the ruse. None of them would, not ever. As thick as the Keyreeves are, they do know the truth of what the key is for, and why the Fairgate was locked to begin with."

"And why is that?" Patience failed to keep the interest out of her voice.

The Marquis gave her an 'I know what you're up to' expression.

"That, Demselle Fell, is a matter far above your place. And besides," he stopped. "We have arrived at your debut. Do exactly what I tell you to do."

## 27. Patience's Debut

Coinquaff and Shivtickle shoved Linus next to Patience. They skulked a few paces in either direction and took up posts. Patience measured the distances in her head; not good. They'd catch her if she ran.

"Are you alright?" she whispered to Linus.

He was too absorbed in staring at the Fair Folk to answer. "Fascinating…"

She was relieved he wasn't hurt, but she wished he would take their dangerous situation more seriously.

"Just look at them!"

She peered across the moon-flooded Fairgate Square. Several cobblemaulers leaned back on their pick hammers and chatted amongst themselves in low voices. The gabledancers were there too, wreathed in a low hum of distant music. Even standing still, they seemed to be dancing. And though she didn't see him, she could tell by the smell the offaltosser was around.

Crowquill was nowhere to be found.

*The Chaos Court-in-Exile.* With a name that fancy, Patience thought it would be a bit more grand than the handful of shadows lurking round the square. There were no more of them than her whole family, if she included her cousins. She was unimpressed.

Linus, on the other hand, was quite taken with the scene.

"There, hovering like a hummingbird—that's a dwindlefilch," Linus said in her ear. "And I think that one, in the ink-stained smock, mumbling to himself, is a quibblemuch."

He sounded breathless as a herd-dog pup trying to sniff every sheep in the field at once. Patience wished she shared his enthusiasm. But fast, furious thoughts of how to stop the Marquis' plans—and the grim image of Shivtickle's finger-knives—drove off any fun she might have felt.

Oblivious to the meagre size of his following, the Marquis marched up onto an over-turned apple crate as if he were surrounded by a crowd of thousands.

"Ladies and gentlemen," he began, striking a noble speech-making pose, "and tossers of offal."

Everyone laughed. It was then that Patience noticed the offaltosser, off in a corner all by himself, none of the other

Fair Folk nearby. His eyes were downcast at his mud-caked shoes. He glanced up. She smiled at him, but he looked quickly away, as if ashamed.

"Tonight, I have the very great pleasure," the Marquis continued, "of introducing someone several of you have already met. From bravely smiting one of our number down on the field of battle—or at least, the alley of scuffle—to waltzing lightly the night away despite being clad in clumsy country clogs..."

He went on and on in that fashion for some time, praising with one side of his mouth and insulting with the other. Linus leaned over and whispered to Patience:

"He's going to make you unlock the gate, isn't he?"

She nodded.

"Give me the key."

His face was dead sincere.

"He just wants the gate opened. If you give me the key, I'm sure he'll let you go."

She shook her head.

"Miss Fell, I insist," he said, trying (without much success) to be high and mighty. "This is not your place. Run on along. I am a Pennywhack after all, kin of the Keyreeves, and that makes this *my* problem."

With a flutter in her stomach, she took his hand and turned back to the grand-standing fox.

"Master Pennywhack," she softly said, "I think there's going to be more than enough of this problem to go round."

The Marquis was wrapping up. He waved her over with one paw.

"What do we do?" Linus asked.

"I don't know."

"Me neither."

She gave his sweaty hand a quick squeeze. "On we go."

"On we go."

The Chaos Court-in-Exile applauded her as she and Linus slowly paced up to the Gate. Everyone that is, except the offaltosser. He seemed as though he would rather be anywhere else. She almost fancied he mouthed the words 'Sorry, Miss,' as she took out the key.

"Demselle Fell, if you will." Reynard-Goupil pointed at the lock.

For one fleeting moment, she imagined flinging the key away, high over everyone's head. But Coinquaff and Shivtickle stood nearby, flexing their enormous muscles.

She unlocked the padlock. The Fairgate rattled. She unhooked the lock and the gate burst open!

A blast of wind that smelled of a million wondrous things knocked her flat on her back. Through the open gate, she saw a wild, vivid, mad landscape. Blazing stars whirled overhead. Impossibly high mountains ringed the horizon, brushed by the lowest stars. Forests of greens deeper than any Patience had ever seen surged up the sides of the mountains, laced through with singing rivers and streams.

The landscape shivered. Dozens of creatures, straight from dreams and nightmares, burst forth from every fold and hollow. They charged towards the Fairgate, a heedless lunatic mob. Their wails, cheers, hoots, howls, cries made a deafening din. They closed in faster than Patience could believe. She rolled out of their way, dragging Linus with her.

"Wait!" He tore himself free of her. He crab-crawled back to grab Crowquill's book, which he'd dropped in the fray.

"Come on!" Patience leapt to her feet. "Now's our chance! Run!"

It was too late. In the time it took for Linus to seize the book and scramble back to her, the horde of creatures from the Chaos Court poured out of the gate and filled the square. There was no room to push through.

The Chaos Court made a half-circle around the open gate. Their cries rose to a crescendo.

At the peak of ruckus, they all went silent at once. The awful quiet frightened Patience more than their wild cacophony.

"What's happening?" Linus whispered.

"The King and the Queen are coming to Court."

The Court all fell to their knees; Linus too. Patience pulled him to his feet.

"They're not *our* King and Queen." She squared her shoulders and faced the gate.

A man and woman in brilliant green robes that shone with their own light stepped through the gate. The man was tall and wore a bow across his back and a quiver of flint arrows by his side. Stag horns protruded from his brow. Woven around them was an oak-and-holly crown. His gaze pierced every creature there, as a hunter marks the fleeing deer.

The woman was ancient and matronly and young by turns, changing age between blinks. She held a staff of living rose-tree that grew and bloomed and withered in rhythm with her shifts. Her eyes seethed with the heedless cruelty of a storm.

"Your Majesties." The Marquis Goupil rose from his bow. "To see you again delights me so."

The King bent his stag-horned brow. "Well done, my soon-to-be son."

"And where is my daughter dear?" the Queen asked.

"My promised bride is not here," the fox said. "She hides in an attic, near."

"She'll never marry you!" Patience shouted. "She loves Johnny Factotum."

At the name 'Factotum' half the Court gasped and half the Court hissed.

The Fair Queen fixed Patience with a gimlet eye. "And who might this ill-mannered child be?"

"She," purred the Marquis, "is the one who, at long last, had the courage to steal the Fairgate Key."

"Since she's been ever so brave and good," the Queen said, raising her rose-tree staff, "let her find her reward in the Ironleaf Wood."

Vines of light and shadow shot out of the staff. They writhed into a sphere around Patience and Linus, trapping the children in a magic cage. With a flick of her wrist, the Fair Queen finished the spell. The cage collapsed. The four corners of Fairgate Square fell off into space and an endless darkness took their place.

## 28. Ironleaf Wood

In the dark, Patience felt Linus' cheek pressed against hers. Their heads nestled into each other's shoulders. Their arms covered each other, shielding them from the Fair Queen's magic. She could hear his heart beat in her temples.

Above them, a bird trilled a little tune.

She lifted her head and opened her eyes. Dim green forest light filtered down into a small clearing, where they knelt. Somewhere, water ran splashing over rocks. The woods felt large and lonely.

"Am I home?"

"That would be very unlikely." Linus stood up. "On the other hand, I've never seen anything like what just happened. So perhaps the unlikely has become extremely likely."

Patience took a deep breath of the forest air. "Smells like home. Like deep in the trees near our farm, where father goes to hunt deer in the fall."

There was a sharp metallic scent in the air too, but she didn't want to worry him by mentioning that. It was probably nothing.

"Oh good!" Linus bent down and retrieved *The Chaos Court*. "I held on to the book. That's something, at least. A place to start."

He brushed the cover off. He sat down cross-legged and began to read.

Patience didn't think that would help much. But she couldn't see how it could hurt. And it would keep him out of trouble while she figured out where they were and how to get back to Whosebourne.

She paced round the clearing. It wasn't at all familiar. That didn't mean much — for all the hours she had spent roaming the woods in the country, there was more of them she hadn't seen than she had. She cupped her hand to her ear to see if she could hear anyone in the distance.

An acorn hit her on the head. It bounced off and hit a rock with a little metal *plink!*

"OW!"

"Patience!" Linus cried, scrambling to his feet. "Are you alright?"

"I'm fine." She rubbed a growing lump on her head. "Go back to reading."

There was a spot of blood on her fingertips. That acorn had been very hard. She scanned the forest floor. She spotted the nut, nestled in a bed of soft moss. She picked it up. It was surprisingly heavy. She turned it around. She nibbled its shell.

It was made of iron.

"Fox in a bon—" she started to say. It sounded wrong. After meeting the Marquis Goupil, she wasn't sure she could ever use that expression again. "It's odd, anyway."

She went to the base of the oak where the acorn had fallen from. Its bark was black and cold. Instead of lichen and moss, clusters of rust grew amid the crannies. She reached up to a low branch to pluck a leaf. Iron.

The whole tree was iron.

She spun in a slow circle. Every tree that ringed the clearing was made of iron—root, branch, leaf, and seed.

"We're not home," she said. "Yours or mine."

Linus mumbled something, deep in his reading.

The forest that had, moments ago, seemed homely and safe, now loomed all round. Patience pictured a hundred hidden dangers amid the warped iron roots and branches.

"A-HA!" crowed Linus.

"WHA!" Patience's heart tried to jump out of her chest and scurry off into the woods.

"Listen to this," he continued, oblivious to the fright he'd given her. "One may demand Challenge of the Fair King by speaking unto Him the Words 'I demand Challenge' thrice — that's three times," he explained, "and upon the Third Speaking, the Fair King must accept the Challenge. Battle then can be done and, for the Victor, a Favor won."

"So?!"

Linus blinked. "It means that if we had demanded challenge back in Fairgate Square and won, we could have asked him to take the Chaos Court out of Town forever as a favor."

Patience clenched her hands into fists to stop them shaking. "So?" she repeated, quietly. "We didn't do that, did we?"

"I guess not. But if we encounter him again and if we demand challenge and if — "

"IF! IF! IF!" Patience yelled. "If ifs were chickens, foxes would feast!"

She had never realized how many of her mother's sayings had to do with foxes.

Linus turned pink. "Yes. I see what you're saying," he mumbled. "Just trying to help." He went from pink to red. He lowered his head. He took off his glasses. He yanked out his shirt tail and began to vigorously clean them. His breath wheezed in his too-narrow nose.

Patience knew she was wrong to be angry with Linus. But that only made her more angry. She wanted to shout that it was stupid to read a book when you were lost in an iron-tree forest in the middle of who knows where; that she needed help, not a school master; that she had had just about enough of his wheezing and glasses.

Fortunately, for their friendship's sake, all that came out was: "GRAH! ARGH! GRAHRAGH!"

She flung her arms in the air. She whirled round and stalked away to the edge of the clearing. She snapped a thin, low-hanging branch off an iron ash. It whistled as she swung it through the air.

That gave her an idea. She gathered a pile of metal twigs. Setting the long, straight branch on the ground, she bunched the twigs round one end. She fished a spare apron string out of her pocket and tied them tightly together. She hoisted her new makeshift broom and gave it a test swing.

"Oh, I'll demand challenge," she murmured to herself with a grimace into the woods.

"Miss Fell?" Linus said.

"Yes?"

"You might want to see this. It's not from the book," he hastened to add.

A single crow perched atop a sapling oak on the other side of the clearing.

"CAW!" She bobbed her head. She pointed her beak at them, then at a narrow path.

"It's mad, but I think she wants us to follow her," Linus said.

"Let's go."

As she strode past him, he touched her arm. "What if it's a trap? Leading to something worse?"

Patience flexed her fingers on her broom. "I almost hope it is."

The crow leapt to another branch and cawed again. She pointed down the path.

Just before they descended into the thick forest, Patience stopped.

"I'm sorry."

"Whatever for?"

His eyes crinkled. He smiled. And, with that, everything was alright again.

## 29. The Ancient Fisher at the Bridge

"It occurs to me," Linus said, lightly touching the sharp edge of a leaf, "that while this forest would be a terrible place to send one of the Fair Folk, it works out quite well for us."

"Why's that?" Patience said, keeping an eye on the bird up ahead.

"The iron trees would very effectively pin them in," he explained, holding a branch out of her way. "Which means that none of the more dangerous ones can get to us."

"The *more* dangerous ones? Aren't they all in town?"

"Not at all! Factotum says in his introduction that the Fair Folk who beleaguer — his word, it means pester — Whosebourne are only a handful of the many, many creatures from the Who-Knows-Where."

"Hrm. Can't say as I like that."

The crow ahead flew off into open sky.

"Hurry!" Linus cried.

"Wait!"

It was too late. He had already charged out of the wood.

"Gosh!" he said, stopping dead in his tracks.

"Be more careful!" She pushed in front of him, with her broom at the ready to defend. "Gosh!" she echoed, when she saw what he had seen.

It was the same vast landscape she had seen through the Fairgate. The sun shone warm and clear overhead, much closer than it should have been. The brilliantly colored country thronged with fields and forest, streams and enormous boulders. Buildings stood here and there, built in shapes that should have fallen down.

"It's never the same," Linus whispered.

She could see what he meant. When she looked away from a part of the scene and looked back, it had changed. Sometimes a little, sometimes a lot. Or at least, she thought it had changed. It got all muddled up in her mind, as if she couldn't hook up what she had seen a moment ago with what she was looking at now.

Except for the mountains; the impossibly tall mountains far, far in the distance that ringed the entire world, brushed by the lowest glow of the sun.

The mountains never moved.

"Down there." Linus pointed.

They stood on a packed-dirt path that led down a hill. At the bottom of the hill a river sparkled. Over the river stretched a bridge. In the middle of the bridge, stood a hunched-over man. He was the only person in view.

"Let me go first," Patience said, brandishing her iron broom.

"That's probably wise."

The man at the bridge was weathered and worn as a thousand-year oak. His bald, brown-speckled pate gleamed in the sun, ringed by a halo of thin white hair. His eyes sat deep in wrinkled sockets. He held a fish pole loosely between two gnarled hands and peered over the railing into the river below. As she approached, Patience noticed the pole did not have a line.

"Sir?"

"Shhhh!" The ancient fisherman raised one crooked finger. It trembled as he pointed down to the water. "Watch. Quiet."

He didn't seem dangerous, but Patience kept her broom ready as she and Linus stepped by his side.

A large brown trout swam in place against the current, basking in the sun-dapple.

"Wh—"

"Shhhh!"

Not wanting to disrespect such an elderly elder (she'd never met anyone so very old), Patience quietly watched the fish. It wriggled side to side, working its fins ever so slightly to stay where it was. It hung suspended in bright, clear water between the air and the pebbled bed. The sight was calming. She slackened her grip on the broom.

"She has no idea we're watching her," the old man said. "And do you ever wonder who," he asked, turning to the children, "might be watching you?"

A crow (perhaps the same one who had led them out of the forest) landed on the old man's shoulder. She cawed once. Spooked, the fish shot off with a great thrash of her tail fin, disappearing into the shadows under the bridge.

"Ah, there's a shame." The old man sighed. He reached up and scratched the crow under her beak. "Not that you're to blame."

"Begging your pardon, sir," Linus interrupted. "Where are we?"

"Ah, my dear Linus! Don't you know?" The fisherman bowed. "Let me be the first to welcome you to the Who-Knows-Where!"

"The what-now?" Patience asked.

"No, not the What-Now. The Who-Knows-Where." In response to their confusion, he elaborated: "The Place that Isn't There. The Ancestral Home of the Folk Most Fair."

"Wait a tick." Linus frowned. "How did you know my name?"

"How do *you* know your name?"

"It's what people call me."

"There you go then," the ancient fisherman said, as if that settled it. "And if he is Linus Pennywhack, that makes you Patience Fell."

"Alright." Patience hoisted the broom-head over her shoulder. "How do you know that? And don't riddle me, or I'll broom you off this bridge."

The old man tottered a little. He raised his open palms. "No need, no need. I'm no offaltosser."

"No," Linus said, slowly. "You're not an offaltosser. You're not any kind of Fair Folk at all. You, sir, are Johnny Factotum."

"Smart boy," the fisherman muttered. "I'm glad she brought you along, for my sake."

"Are you sure it's him?" Patience asked Linus, not taking her eyes off the old man nor lowering her broom.

"Not *completely* sure," he said. "These days I'm not certain of anything. I mean, if you had asked me if I was sure a queen from behind a locked iron gate could send me to a place where the sun was too close and the landscape shifted whenev—"

"Linus!"

"Right. Sorry. Get to the point." He cleared his throat like a schoolmaster about to give a lecture. "Point the first: He is here—wherever here is—through the Fairgate. Point the second: The crows can come and go freely between Whosebourne and this place. Point the third: Crowquill has been sending messages to Johnny Factotum through the Fairgate via the birds. Oh!"

He slapped his forehead.

"What?"

"I just put that together. Crowquill. Crows."

Patience growled.

"Sorry, sorry." Linus hastily finished his explanation. "If she has been writing notes to Factotum, she must have told him about us, which would explain why he knows who we are. And since this agéd gentleman—"

"—too kind," murmured the ancient fisherman.

"—knows about us, he is probably Johnny Factotum."

Patience thought that through. She couldn't disagree. But she still didn't trust the strange old man, not any further than she could throw the Keyreeve.

"How did you get here, then?"

"Aye," he replied, "there's a tale long in the telling, and better for my bones to be a-sitting. Come, to my home."

Even in a normal place, Patience knew better than to accept an invitation from a stranger. And that went at least double in the Who-Knows-Where.

"If you please, Mister Factotum," she said, trying to be polite but firm, "we'd best stay here."

"Of course." Factotum eased himself into an over-stuffed leather chair. "And here is where we shall stay."

Patience blinked. The bridge and river were gone. She and Linus now stood in a cozy library, walled with books from floor to ceiling and carpeted with cast-off scraps of scribbled-over paper. All of the pages were covered in Crowquill's large loopy-lettered writing.

"Do have a seat," Factotum held out a plate of cookies. "Can I offer you something to eat?"

# 30. Factotum's Tale

Patience closed her eyes and pricked her ears. The sound of the river was gone and the smell of fresh air too. Crowquill's notes rustled under her feet. The room smelled musty and dusty — the way a well-used library should be. There was no doubt. They really were there.

As much as 'really' meant anything in the Who-Knows-Where, she guessed.

Linus thumped his knuckles against the books (every one of which was a copy of *The Chaos Court*). "How did you do it? Was it the light on the water that you used to mesmerize us, so we wouldn't remember walking here? Some sort of mirror-dazzling or animal magnetism?"

"I don't know what any of that means." Factotum took a sip from a cup of tea. He held out the plate of cookies again. Wisps of delicious steam rose from them.

"Stop that!" Linus' face got red. "Stop pretending to do impossible things!"

Patience put a hand on his arm. "It's alright."

"No, it isn't alright! Not a bit alright!" He waved his arms around. "Things either are a certain way or they're not. You walk from a bridge to a library, passing through everything in between. He can't just muddle that all up and act like nothing's wrong!"

He was on the verge of tears. Patience had no idea how to make things better. She patted him on the shoulder. "There, there," she said. "There. There."

She couldn't remember ever having felt, or been, more awkward.

His lips screwed up all crooked. His eyes wobbled in their sockets. He dropped his head. His shoulders began to shake.

"There," she tried again. "There, there."

"No, no," he gasped. "No more!"

He was laughing!

"No more," he kept on. "Please stop!" He hunched over, wheezing *khee khee khee khee*.

Patience had no idea what was so funny. She was concerned he had gone mad. She wasn't sure she could escape this strange place *with* his help, but she was certain she couldn't if he'd lost his mind.

"Oh, Miss Fell," he said at last. He took off his glasses and wiped them clean. "You are the bravest, cleverest, strongest person I have ever met. But you are terrible, just *terrible* at making people feel better."

"Pfft! You!" She gave him a little swat with her broom. She was relieved he was laughing and embarrassed that he had said all those nice things and just a touch irked that he'd worried her so.

He blew out a long breath. "Whew! Thank you for reminding me I was being silly. And now, Mr. Factotum, that we've got that sorted out, I think it's time you explain some things."

"Very well," Factotum said.

In her concern for her friend, Patience had almost forgotten the old man was there.

"You!" she said, abandoning manners. "Put away those cookies and get us home!"

The cookies were nothing more than crumbs in the old man's beard. He set the empty plate on the ground by his chair.

"Home?" he said. "In order to find your way home, you first must know where you are."

"And where exactly is that?" Patience asked. "And don't give us a bunch of rhyming riddles and call that an answer. Plain talk, if you please."

"You are a very impertinent child," Factotum said. "It will probably get you far."

Patience wasn't sure he'd said something nice, but she decided to curtsy as if he had.

"It's been a long time since I've been in the world," he went on. "Do children of a certain age still have to leave home and find their place?"

"Yes, sir," Linus said. "Or they are sent there, if everyone already knows what their place is supposed to be."

"Then think of this," he waved his arm, "as my place. But not the place I left home to find. This is place I made myself, to have somewhere better to go than the place I found."

"Riddles," Patience muttered, with a vicious whisk at the papers at her feet.

"Peace, peace." Factotum held up his hands. "I'll explain."

He settled back into his chair. He gazed past the children, to the long ago and far away.

"I didn't have to go far to find my place in the world. I was born poorer than poor in Whosebourne. My place was, and always would be, the alleys and the gutters. I knew that as soon as I knew anything. My ending was written right from the start."

"Chaos claps in the beat of your heart..." Patience murmured.

Factotum tapped the side of his nose. "Exactly."

"Then how did you become a famous author?" Linus asked.

"Maybe not so famous," Factotum said. "You'd probably never heard of me before Miss Fell came knocking at your door, had you?"

Linus blushed. "Sorry."

"Never mind that. Fame's a waste. But you're right about one thing. No one would have expected a street scamp like me to amount to much of anything. We—my mates and I—lived catch as catch can, stealing for food and whatever else we might want. And at the end of the day, if we'd gotten lucky and weren't too hungry, we'd lay back on a rooftop with the crows and I'd tell tales that would make us forget our place for a while."

Patience was surprised to see a tear glint in his eye.

"For all we were hungry and dirty," he explained, "those weren't bad days. Sometimes even good enough I miss them. Me and my best mate Aldo—"

"Aldo?" Linus interrupted. "You don't mean Aldo Pennywhack?"

"One and the same."

"You mean to tell me that my great-great-and-a-few-more-greats-grandfather, First Keyreeve of Whosebourne was a poor street boy?!"

"And what's wrong with that?" Patience asked.

"It's just—I mean, that is—of course, if—nothing wrong, but—" Linus flustered out a few more half-sentences before finishing, "It's not what the history books say."

"You can't trust everything someone wrote in a book," Factotum said. "I should know."

Linus grumbled something inaudible.

"My point exactly."

"That's what Reynard said!" Patience exclaimed. She explained. "Not the part about books. He told me that two hundred years ago, the first Keyreeve was common as me."

"Ah, the Marquis Goupil," said Factotum. "My most troublesome creation. But every story needs a villain, I suppose. Keeps the heroes on their toes."

"Your creation?!" the children cried in unison.

"It seems," the old man said, stroking his beard, "that I've gotten ahead of myself. Perhaps that's for the best. Yes."

He leaned forward. His eyebrows bristled. His voice dropped deep and serious. "Time to hurry my tale along. The sand scatters round, and the hour grows short."

*The King and the Queen,* Patience thought, *are already at Court.*

## 31. The Start of the Chaos Court

"Yes," Factotum continued, in answer to their curious stares. "I created Reynard, the Marquis Goupil. And Miss Crowquill and the rest of the Chaos Court. All the Fair Folk you've met or might ever meet, from the appletipper to the zephyrweft, are the children of my mind."

"Explain," Linus curtly demanded.

"I wish I could," Factotum said. "But I'll have to settle for telling you what happened.

"As I said, I used to tell stories for my mates, to keep us happy and help us not notice how hungry we were. The first time was when Aldo and I were hiding in an alley. We'd just stolen a pie from a window sill. A great wind blew through and the trash whirled all round us. Meanwhile, the baker was nearby, cursing us with every word he knew.

"I was in a funny mood. 'Watch out! An offaltosser!' I whispered to Aldo. He stuffed his fist in his mouth to stifle a laugh. I kept on about how they turned into whirlwinds and swore terrible swears. When I described the stink, Aldo couldn't stand it and burst out laughing. That led the baker right to us. We stuffed as much of the pie as we could in our mouths, and scrambled away as he broom-whacked the seat of our pants."

"Serves you right," Patience said. "For stealing."

Factotum chuckled. "I suppose so."

He continued his story: "Later that night, Aldo asked me to tell our little group about the offaltosser. So I did, adding more to the tale. And I threw in the cobblemaulers, to explain a carriage with a broken wheel we'd seen earlier in the day.

"Before long, the story spread, as stories do. My friends would tell their friends, who would tell people I didn't even know. No one could tell it as well as me, though. So more and more people sought me out to hear it from the source.

"When new people came, Aldo would introduce me. He would go on and on about how hungry I was, and how I could barely get through a story without a bite to eat. I'd put on quite the show of being weak. It worked! People we had stolen from not a week earlier just *gave* us the food we would have nicked. Even the foul-mouthed baker chipped in a mince meat pie.

"Of course, I couldn't just tell the one story about the offaltosser, over and over. To keep people happy — because happy people are more likely to share what they have — I made up new stories about new creatures, every day. I borrowed from all around town. A hole in the roof must have been caused by a gabledancer's hoof. A missing purse? Pinched twixt a dwindlefilch's fingers. A drunkard's empty money-bag? Coinquaff struck again. You get the idea.

"Life was good. We had so much food coming in, we could even spare some for the crows.

"Then one day a very fancy man in a red silk coat came to watch me tell a story. He was the kind of man who created space around him, just by being so fancy. And when I was done, he gave me a gold coin and told me to wash my face and be at the Lord Mayor's Estate first thing in the morning."

Patience could imagine how out-of-place little Factotum must have felt. She remembered her first visit to Pennywhack Manor and the Keyreeve's nasty comments about how dirty she was.

"To hasten on," he continued, "word of my stories had reached even the Lord Mayor. He made me stand in his grand hall, hands clasped behind my back, and tell him all my stories. It was a long day. But at the end of it, he gave me a little room in his house. I even convinced him to let Aldo stay with me. I had found a new place in the world, and quite a pleasant place it was."

"But how does any of that relate to the real Chaos Court?" Linus asked. "The ones who sent us here and who are, I assume, tearing apart the town while we waste our time here?"

"They became real from his stories," Patience said. "Right?" she asked Factotum.

Linus frowned. "That's not how things work. Things aren't real just because people believe in them."

"Coins," Factotum said. "Countries. Crimes. The ineffable efficacy of grace."

Patience had no idea what the last one meant, but she was pretty sure she understood what the old storyteller was getting at. Coins and countries and crimes only existed because lots of people agreed they should.

"I think that's exactly what happened," she said to Linus.

"Hrmph."

"Ten years went by," Factotum said, ignoring Linus' grumbling. "Ten good years, I must say. Aldo and I toured the world, telling my stories on street corners and in packed theatres. The Lord Mayor even ordered them printed up in little collections.

"We were coming home late one afternoon. I was half-asleep, worn out from talking for weeks on end. As we passed by an alleyway, I saw a whirlwind of trash. When I blinked, all the garbage dropped. A tiny offaltosser stood in its place. He smiled right at me, gave me a wink, said a few things I won't repeat, and whooshed off down the road.

"I would have thought I was dreaming, but Aldo saw the same thing. Neither one of us wanted to be the first to admit it, so we pretended it hadn't happened.

"Until the gabledancers woke us up the next night, stomping the rooftop full of holes. And the cobblemaulers put a pit in the middle of our street so big a deer couldn't jump it—we watched them do it, from the safety of our window, with their little hammers, searching for their eggs just like I had made up."

"I don't believe it," Linus said, his arms folded over his chest.

"Neither do I," Factotum replied. "But it happened anyway."

## 32. The First Keyreeve

Linus harrumphed again.

"I have a lengthy list of objections to your narrative."

Patience shushed him. She didn't know whether or not the story was true, but she wanted to hear how it ended. She leaned her broom on a bookcase. She sat down cross-legged.

"Go on."

"I don't mean to make the sudden appearance of the Fair Folk sound all bad," Factotum said. "After all, we did get to listen to Madam Zephyrweft sing her windy song on the spring evening. And Jack Appletipper was good for a laugh, for everyone except the fruit-seller of course. And there was Miss Crowquill…"

"You loved her," Patience said.

"How could you possibly know that?" Linus demanded.

"Listen to the way he says her name."

"I did," Factotum confessed. "And I still do, though I've gotten so very old here and she has remained the same."

"Because you wrote it that way, right?" Linus said with a skeptical twist of his lips. "That the Fair Folk don't age?"

A sad shadow darkened Factotum's face.

"Sorry." Linus sounded as if he meant it, for all his suspicion about the old man's story.

Factotum's wrinkles crinkled into a soft and wistful smile. "No worries. A valuable lesson—be careful what stories you tell. You never know when you'll have to face them in the flesh.

"And yes, I made up Miss Crowquill because I was lonely. Aldo was a good mate, the best friend a man could want. But I'd reached the age where I wanted someone to sing songs to and write poems for and to blush and fluster when she answered me back."

"Why did you make her so mad?" Patience asked.

"I didn't mean to. I thought it would be quite romantic—the damsel high in her attic, sending messages out by crow and waiting for the brave young man to rescue her."

Now it was Patience's turn to harrumph.

"I know, I know," Factotum said. "Now, at least, I know how stupid-silly that is. Back then, I was as young as you, but near as wise. But to return to my story.

"The Fair Folk were wrecking the town, Miss Crowquill and a handful of others excepted. The Lord Mayor and all his men were powerless to stop them. No one could keep a roof over their head or a street under their feet. Something had to be done. Finally, the Lord Mayor came up with a plan.

"Unfortunately, his plan was to load up everything he could carry and move to a different country. That left the rest of us in the midst of a mess. Since they were my stories, I knew I had to clean things up."

"And yet, here we are," Linus said.

"So it would seem." Factotum winked at him. "Truth be told, it wasn't me who really knew I had to clean things up. I wanted to run. I was all ready to take Miss Crowquill by the hand and flee fast as we could to another land. It was your great-great-many-times-great grandfather Aldo who set me straight.

"'Johnny,' he said, 'stop your packing. Alleys or palaces, Whosebourne is our place in the world and I'm not going to let anyone, real or Fair, tear it to bits. I have a plan.'"

"The Fairgate," Patience said.

"Exactly," Factotum said. "He was always smarter than me, Aldo. He'd read through all my stories and remembered every detail—including the Fair Folk's weakness to iron. And the Marquis Goupil's quest to be King."

"By marrying Miss Crowquill!" Linus exclaimed.

"I thought you didn't believe the story," Patience said.

"I don't," Linus said. "Not a word of it. Completely implausible. But, that said, if the Marquis Goupil would be King, what better way to get there than marrying the King's daughter? And he did say, back in Fairgate Square, that was exactly what he planned to do."

"That's something, anyway," Factotum said, satisfied.

"Why would you want that?" Patience asked.

"I don't. But if there is to be a wedding, that buys us a little bit of time before they really tear into it."

Patience had been so caught up in his story that she had forgotten about the town and the Chaos Court who was, even now, wreaking havoc on every street and home. She leapt to her feet and seized her broom.

"We have to get back!"

"Please," Factotum said. "Indulge an old man for just a few moments longer. I haven't had the chance to tell my story in two hundred years."

Patience stayed standing.

"It may explain a thing or two," Factotum continued. "Maybe you'll learn something to help chase off the Fair Folk?"

"He makes a good point," Linus interjected. "More knowledge is always good."

Patience noticed that for someone who didn't believe a word of the story, Linus was pretty keen on getting every detail. She held her tongue about that, though. She sat back down.

"I'll be quick and even quicker," Factotum said. "Aldo had me finally tell the story about how the Marquis Goupil was promised the hand of the Atticmad. And the key point was that the wedding must take place in the Who-Knows-Where — the magical land I'd invented to be the Fair Folk's home. It was reachable only through a hole in the air, in what we then called the Fairfolk Square.

"While the Chaos Court prepared for the marriage, Aldo secretly had a blacksmith forge an iron gate and lock and key."

"Hold on," Patience interrupted. "You were just going to let Reynard marry the woman you loved?"

"Hardly," Factotum replied. "I was to sneak into the Who-Knows-Where and wait in the Ironleaf Wood till the right moment. Then I would ride pell-mell into the wedding party, seize Crowquill, and beat a retreat through the hole in the air back to town. The moment we jumped through, Aldo would slam the Fairgate and lock it tight."

"I can't help but observe," Linus said, "that you are on this side of the gate and the Marquis and several others remained on the other side."

"The story got away from us."

Factotum rolled his eyes at his own folly.

"The Marquis was more clever than I'd given him credit for. Even for someone I made up. He knew Miss Crowquill was dread-afraid of the great outdoors. So on the wedding day, he convinced her to hide in her attic and he left a few followers in Whosebourne to make sure she stayed put. He put on the bride's veil himself and stood by the King and Queen's side.

"When I thundered up on a tame nightmare, I had no idea it was him. I scooped him into my arms. Pursued by almost the whole Chaos Court, we fled like mad across the Who-Knows-Where—not so different from the boy running from the baker with a stolen pie.

"As my horse leapt towards the Gate, the Marquis shoved me off. I tumbled end-over-end across the Who-Knows-Where as he spurred the horse on to town.

"Aldo, seeing the bride astride the mare pass by, slammed the iron door and locked the iron lock for good. The Marquis disappeared. I was trapped behind the Fairgate. Aldo was a hero. The rest, you know as history."

"No," Linus said. "We most certainly do not. None of the histories tell any of this."

Factotum winked. "We did have to take a few liberties in the official reports."

"We?"

"I discovered the crows could come and go as they please, giving me a way to reach my friend and my love. So though I was out of Whosebourne, I wasn't completely out of the loop. Once Aldo became the first Keyreeve, I advised him to do everything he could to suppress my stories. I thought maybe if everyone forgot them, if no one believed, the Fair Folk themselves would disappear."

"It didn't work," Patience said. "It didn't work."

"It was worth a try," Factotum said with a shrug. "At least there weren't any new ones created."

"That's why the Keyreeves decide what gets printed," Linus said. "And why my uncle had those copies of your book!"

"Every Keyreeve since Aldo has known the importance of keeping those stories hidden." He waved at the shelves filled with copies of *The Chaos Court*. "Under cover of dark, the Keyreeve stuffs the books through the Fairgate for me to collect. And no one is allowed to tell the tales themselves."

"But it didn't," Patience repeated, "WORK!"

## 33. Factotum's Farewell

"It didn't work," Patience said a fourth time. She repeated herself with mounting fury. "It didn't work, it didn't work, it didn't work."

She had stood up and grabbed her broom again. She jabbed the head of it at Factotum to emphasize every word.

"All your lies, all the secrets, all the hiding, all of the clever grown-up tricks! None of it worked! Everything you did, and we're still stuck with a town torn down by Fair Folk, just like before. You and your stories made a great big mess of my place in the world!"

"Yes." The old man rose from his big leather chair with a series of heavy grunts. "You're right."

She stopped. She was taken aback. A grown-up had never agreed with her when she was angry before.

"All of our plans failed, in one way or another. Aldo died and the real meaning behind the Keyreeve's office was lost to time. Crowquill hid in her attic, waiting for a savior who would never come. And in the end all I could do was watch and wait and trade letters by crow and hope that someone brave and true would come along to do what I couldn't do."

"How convenient for you," Patience snapped. "Would've been nice to have been asked first. Or at all." She felt used and she did not like the feeling.

"You've inherited a wicked thicket, no mistake. And none of it would have happened if those of us who came before were a little less clever—or a great deal more. But," and here Factotum's eyebrows bristled, "there's no changing what's true, so what are *you* going to do?"

Put on the spot that way, Patience wasn't sure what to say.

"The first thing," Linus said, all business and resolution, "is we have to get back to Whosebourne. Is that even possible? It should be, in theory, since the Fairgate is opened."

Factotum smiled at him. "We hoped for one strong child to help and we get two."

A cacophonic chorus of caws rose from all sides. The din grew so loud, the children had to cover their ears.

When the crow-calls were done, Patience saw the library had fallen away. They stood high on a mountain.

The whole of the Who-Knows-Where stretched out at their feet. Rows upon rows of crows perched all round them. A hole in the air wavered at the rocky tip-top of the peak.

"It's time," Factotum said, with a weary sigh. Stoop-backed, he shuffled up behind them. "It's time you went home and set the world to rights."

"Aren't you coming with us, sir?" Linus asked. All traces of his skepticism were gone.

"Me? I'm afraid not. After two hundred years, my time is long past done. Even the magic of the Who-Knows-Where can't keep a mortal man upright forever. It's your story now."

"We'll do our best, sir. With whatever's left. Let's go, Patience." Linus picked a careful path across the slippery stones towards the hole in the air.

Realizing what Factotum was saying, Patience couldn't stay angry with him any more. She curtsied, deep as she could.

"I'll let Miss Crowquill know," she said, "if I see her again."

The audience of birds ruffled their feathers and murmured.

"She'll know," the old man said. "Besides, she deserves better than being the romantic fantasy of a young man who will never be again. She deserves her own place in the world. And with courage, maybe she'll find it."

"I'll make sure she does," Patience said. "I promise!"

She did not move. She had one more question. It wasn't a question that made any sense, but if there was anywhere in the world to ask it, anywhen it might be answered, it was here and it was now.

"Why me?"

"'The sighting of this filthy wee man and the hearing of his curses is therefore said to be most unlucky,'" Factotum quoted his own book about the offaltosser.

"That's it? I'm just unlucky?"

The storyteller wasn't done. He continued, quoting the part Patience had never gotten to read, the part covered with leek sauce. "'However, if you are kind enough to care for this foul fellow, then you will always choose to make your world a better place and you will always find a way.'"

"You were brave to stand your ground on your first day in town," Factotum said. "And strong to fight back when things got strange. But more than all that, when that stinky little body lay knocked out on the ground, you went to his side and you *cared*."

The wind howled far below. The Who-Knows-Where shuddered all round. Factotum waved her on to Whosebourne.

"Quick now! Out you go, Patience Fell. Do your job, and do it well."

When she got to the Fairgate, she turned back one last time. The ancient storyteller saluted. The crows took to wing, dimming the sun with their pitch-black flock.

The wild mountain wind whipped up the cliffside. It caught the old man in its grip. It flung him round and round. His gray, bent, withered body shook into dozens, scores, hundreds of paper pages. They flew up in a funnel. The whirlwind danced over the edge of the cliff. Factotum's final pages dispersed the length and breadth of the Who-Knows-Where, covering every inch of the mad land in prosy snow.

Dashing a tear from her eye with the back of her hand, Patience stepped through the hole in the air into Fairgate Square.

## 34. Patience Faces a Terrible Mess

Sun streamed down into the square. Hours had passed, maybe days. Patience tapped the cobbles with her iron broom. They were really there. Cries and rumbles echoed in the distance, from everywhere.

"Alright. Whatever it is, it's still going on," she said. "Let's—"

She did not get to finish. Coinquaff and Shivtickle stepped out of an alcove.

"Brruhp," Coinquaff said. "What do you know? The boss was right."

Shivtickle flexed his fingers. He never took his eyes off her. "He was."

"Good thing he left us here to keep an eye out. I was mad sore about missing the fun, but this will be just as good."

"Stay behind me," Patience said to Linus. She stepped forward. She brandished her broom.

"Of course," Coinquaff continued, lurching closer to her, "this means I lost a purse to Dandyhandler. He said the girl'd be clever enough to get back. I guess I'd better make this worth that lost coin."

"Either of you takes another step closer," Patience said, "and you're getting it."

Shivtickle laughed a nasty laugh. His fingers turned into boney knives. They grated on one another with a shivering sound.

"I ain't no offaltosser, girl."

He lunged at her, blades flashing in the sun.

She swung the iron-twig broom hard as she could. She hit the thug right across his chin.

A blue flash filled Fairgate Square. The smell of after-lightning filled the air.

Shivtickle bellowed. The terrible deep sound got smaller and higher. He deflated like a balloon. He shrank and shrank and shrank, until he was nothing more than a wee, squeaking speck. He hopped around like a flea until he fell into a crack in the sidewalk and was gone.

"You want to go next?" Patience said to Coinquaff. Her heart thundered in her ears.

Coinquaff drew himself up. All his drunken swaying vanished. He narrowed evil eyes at her and flexed his fingers into fists.

He turned and ran as fast as he could in the other direction.

Patience chased him to the edge of the square, broom raised over her head.

"That's right!" she yelled after him. "Tell Goupil I'm coming for him and I have a brand-new broom!"

She shook her head back and laughed madly at the sky.

Linus stood stock-still, utterly flummoxed. He didn't even have the presence of mind to investigate the spot in the cobbles where Shivtickle had disappeared.

Patience twirled her broom. She curtsied.

Linus blinked. He bowed back.

"R-remarkable," he said, as if the word weren't even close to enough, but it was all he had.

"Oh, I'm just getting started."

From where she stood, she could see gabledancers kicking roofs to bits. A dandyhandler shook a rich man down for his silks and rings. Two dozen cobblemaulers pried up an entire street. A swarm of fluttering dwindlefilches robbed the running market crowd blind.

The Chaos Court had come back to town and they were tearing the whole place down.

"What are we going to do?" Linus asked.

Patience hefted her iron-whisked broom and glared at the mess.

"I'm going to do what I do best."

## 35. Chaos Comes to Pennywhack Manor

With Linus behind her, Patience swept her way across Town. One by one, the Fair Folk fled before her, or else went down.

During a break in the fight, Linus asked: "Do you have a plan?"

"The Manor," Patience gasped. She could barely catch her breath. This was harder work than she'd ever worked.

"Of course," Linus said. "It's the perfect place for a wedding."

Patience tapped her nose. She hoisted her broom with burning arms and waded once more into the fray.

When they reached Pennywhack Manor, they ducked down behind an overturned carriage. They took a moment to regroup. Patience peeked up to spy out the scene.

The roof had nearly been danced off. The courtyard had been cobble-mauled to bare dirt. Smoke rose from every chimney at once. Garbage flew from every window, with bits of splintered furniture mixed in. Fair Folk clung to every crevice and crennel.

"Sneak round the side?" Linus asked. "Slip in behind the walls?"

Patience stood up in full view. "I've had enough of that. I'm good enough for the front door."

"That you are." Linus stepped to her side. "Let's go."

He brandished the last copy of Factotum's book. It looked much the worse for wear.

"Have you been whacking with that this whole time?" Patience asked as they marched up the wide front stairs.

"It's surprisingly effective."

He illustrated the point by knocking a dwindlefilch out of the air into the rose bushes.

"Nice!"

Linus gave her a curtsy. One quick laugh between them, and then they were back to business.

They each grabbed one of the enormous two-story front doors. They shoved with all their might.

The Great Hall had been transformed almost beyond recognition. Vines and branches knit together to make two great living thrones at the center of the room. Music rose from the broken stones of the once-magnificent marble floor. The townspeople, Fancy and Plain, cowered in the corners, while the finer Fair Folk stood in wait.

High on their thrones, the King and Queen held court in lofty glory. Beneath them, a few steps down, a veiled Crowquill and the Marquis Goupil, in Reynard form.

A dwindlefilch in a bishop's hat raised one hand.

"Dearly beloved..." he began the wedding ceremony.

Before Patience could deal with that, Linus jabbed her in the ribs.

"Over there," he whispered in a panic.

Through the shattered dining room doors, Patience spotted the Keyreeve. He'd been trussed up on a spit, over a large fire. A quivering, drooling man in a stained smock slowly turned him over the flames.

"One thing at a time," she murmured to Linus. "He'll be fine."

Linus ignored her. He lunged towards his uncle. Patience grabbed his arm.

"They're just hotting him up to scare him." She held his eyes with all the seriousness in her. "Trust me. I've been that close to the fire plenty of times."

Reluctantly, Linus nodded. "You know what to do?"

"Oh yes."

"Three times?"

"I remember."

Patience squared her shoulders. She stiffened her lips. Everything in the room faded except the Marquis Goupil and a great red cloud of rage.

"OI!" Her voice echoed throughout the Great Hall.

The music stopped.

The King and Queen lifted their heads. The Marquis glared over his shoulder. The Chaos Court all turned towards the lone kitchen girl, armed with nothing but bravery and a broom.

In a firm, steady voice, Patience said just three words:

"I demand challenge."

## 36. Patience Demands Challenge

Patience stepped into the middle of a bigger hush than she had ever heard. Everyone stared at her. After what felt like a hundred years, the Horned King broke the silence.

"Say it but once," he chanted, "and it were never said."

"I demand challenge," Patience said again.

The Fair Queen rose from her throne. She lifted her writhing-vine staff. "Say it but twice, and we'll have your head."

"I demand challenge," Patience said once more, quiet, but solid as the mountains that circled the Who-Knows-Where.

"Say it thrice," the entire Chaos Court intoned, "and the King stands challengéd."

The King stood. "And who among you will stand in my stead?"

"What?" Patience muttered.

"The King can't fight for himself," Linus whispered. "By custom, he needs a champion."

"I know who I'm hoping for," she growled.

She was not disappointed.

The Marquis Goupil stepped down away from Crowquill. "My Father-to-be, I will dispatch this common serving girl. As beneath me," he said, turning back into a fox, "as biting her will be."

"And who will serve as your second, Marquis?"

"That's a back-up, in case you fall or can't finish the fight," Linus explained.

No one said anything. Everyone eyed Patience's iron broom.

"Not a lot of friends now, eh Reynard?" Patience said.

The Marquis glared at Coinquaff, who was trying (unsuccessfully) to hide behind a slender gabledancer. The thug shuffled up.

"I'll do it," he mumbled.

"And I will stand with Patience," Linus said, loud and clear.

The way he said it muddled Patience all up again. She pushed the tangle of feelings off to one side. She didn't need the distraction.

"The seconds are set," the Queen said. "Now what are the stakes?"

"If she lives but fails," Goupil said, "she becomes part of the Chaos Court."

The Queen laughed cruelly. "That's an honor, not a penalty."

The Marquis bowed. "I did not finish, my Queen. She becomes part of the Chaos Court... as the offaltosser's bride." He smirked. "When she is of marriageable age, of course."

The Hall erupted in laughter. A few of the cobblemaulers winked at the offaltosser and gave him a thumbs up. The smelly wee man stared down at his boots. He shrank into the corner.

"I'd rather be an offaltosser's wife than any one of you," Patience said. "At least he's honest to what he does, and true."

The offaltosser scuffed his heels. He mutter something quite dreadful—but in a nice way.

"So mote it be," the King said. "If you live, but fail, you will be married to the offaltosser."

"We can make it a double wedding," the Queen purred, with a nasty twist of her upper lip.

"And when I win?" Patience said.

"And if you win?" the King replied.

She jabbed the point of her broom at the Marquis. "He goes in the Gate to the Who-Knows-Where. And as for the rest of you—"

She stopped.

She spotted the offaltosser, off by himself. He didn't really deserve to be banished from the world. Then she remembered how joyous the gabledancers' dance was. And how the cobblemaulers were searching for their kin, not really tearing up the streets on purpose. Some of the Fair Folk were wicked, sure, like Coinquaff and Shivtickle, but others were just living their lives and tending to their businesses. Just like everyone.

She couldn't stand in the way of that. But she couldn't have them tear down her town.

"—and as for the rest of you," she said, "when I win, you will leave Whosebourne and its Plain Folk alone, and find a place in the world all your own."

"Done!" the King said. "'Tis time to fight. Let the battle decide what's right."

He clapped his broad hunter's hands three slow times.

Pennywhack Manor fell away to all four sides.

## 39. Patience Fights to the Finish

Patience and Linus stood in one corner of Fairgate Square. The Marquis and Coinquaff were opposite them. The King and Queen sat enthroned on a dais. All around them, from the roofs and balconies, down to the curbs, Folks Fair and Plain gathered to watch the duel.

"Patience," Linus said.

"Yes?"

"As your second—" He stopped. He took a big gulp and a deep breath. "As your second, I can stand in for you. You don't need to fight."

Across the square, Patience could see the Marquis arguing fiercely with Coinquaff. The brute finally crossed his arms, shook his head, and stood his ground.

She turned back to Linus. He was so earnest, with his thick glasses and his hair all mussed. She kissed him on the cheek. He got very, very red.

"You're brave enough, fancy man," she said. "But you wouldn't know the first thing to do with the business end of a good broom."

She faced the field of battle. She raised her broom in salute. The Marquis bared his teeth.

The Fair King waved his hand. The air was torn by the clang of a gong. The fight was on.

Patience sprinted across the square, hoping to end it quick. Goupil leapt nimbly aside. He scampered to her corner. She spun on her heel and held up the broom in defense.

They circled one another around the hole in the air. They got closer and closer with every side-ways step.

Suddenly, the Marquis faked a snap to Patience's left. He jumped right. That fooled her just enough that he nipped a rip in her sleeve.

She lunged out with the same great whack that had sent the offaltosser into the alley wall. Goupil was too fast for that. He rolled under her feet. That tripped her up. As they tumbled together, he bit her wrist.

The crowd roared.

"First blood!" the King thundered.

It was a shallow bite, but it still dripped a bit. Patience wiped her hands on her apron, so as not to get her broom-handle slick with blood.

Goupil went left again, but this time, she was ready. She dodge right, swinging at his belly as he jumped over her. The wind from the broom ruffled his fur, but she didn't connect.

Her wrist throbbed. The Marquis was good. Perhaps too good for her. And his teeth could kill.

She pictured herself surrendering and becoming an offaltosser's wife. The fox sensed her distraction. He bounced off of her chest, taking a hard bite on her shoulder.

The Fair Folk stomped and cheered for their King's champion. The Plain Folk wailed and booed.

"Time out, time out!" Linus yelled, but the din of the crowd swallowed up his plea.

Patience pressed her shoulder and winced. She backed up to Linus.

"Any ideas?"

She couldn't hear his reply. She ran at the fox again. This time, she pretended to stumble right before she got to him. She hoped to fake him into pouncing and catch him broadsides with the iron twigs.

He was too clever.

He came in low. He grabbed her ankle and pulled. She cried out, fell for real, and, worse, lost hold of the broom.

It flew skittering into the crowd. The Fair Folk parted around it, like it was a poisonous snake.

Patience reached out her hands for her weapon. It might as well have been on the moon.

The Marquis paced slowly back and forth on the far side of the square. He waved up the crowd, who shouted "Blood! Blood! Blood!"

With one cut of his paw, he silenced them.

"Only now, Demselle Fell," he purred, "do you realize how small you truly are."

He charged.

Everything slowed down.

Patience had all the time in the world to think about her family back in the country. They would be so sad. She thought about Miss Alys, who had been so gruff and so kind. She thought about Whosebourne, her place in the world, and how she'd failed to save it. She wished she could have kissed Linus once for real, instead of a peck on the cheek.

Her arm and shoulder and ankle hurt so badly. She wondered if Factotum had hurt when he'd died. It didn't seem so.

The fox leapt. His razor fangs glinted in the sun.

Movement drew her eye away from death, to her broom on the empty cobbles.

A whirlwind surged out of the crowd. A swirling mass of trash. It lifted the broom up and flung it across the square. The storm collapsed. The tiny offaltosser crouched in its place, blowing on his smoking hands.

The broom tumbled end over end, right into her hands.

She swung it hard as she could. She caught the fox on his haunches mid-pounce. Her shoulders shuddered from the shock of the blow. Every muscle screamed.

A blue burst of lightning blinded her. A bright after-image of a fox tumbled through the darkness behind her eyes and disappeared.

She couldn't believe she'd won.

She passed out.

## 40. Patience Rewarded

She woke in a strange bed. It was too nice for *The Crock and Dice*. There was a thick, soft comforter and a deep-stuffed straw-tick mattress. She smelled flowers through the window and heard morning birds. For the briefest instant, she thought she was back in the country.

She sat up.

"Oof!" She nearly passed out again. She hurt in more ways than she thought possible. Her every muscle burned. Amid that common throb, sharp points stabbed in her wrist, her shoulder, her ankle, and her neck. She reached up to her throat and felt a bandage there.

"He must've gotten me and I didn't even notice."

"He did," Linus said from beside the bed. "For all the good it did him."

"Oi! You! Linus!"

She remembered how her last thought had been about kissing him. She blushed crimson.

He didn't seem to notice.

"Good to see you awake, Miss Fell. I'm not much of a nurse," he held up a book, "but Paracelsus here knows a thing or two."

"We won?"

"That we did. After you knocked the fox tail-over-bonnet into the Fairgate, I ran over and locked it again. The Horned King waved his hands and the whole Chaos Court vanished."

He frowned. "I still can't explain that part. And I don't know where they went. Among other things."

"How's the town? Did they wreck it too badly?"

"The damage was less than we had feared. You and I saw the worst of it during our battle to the Manor. Most of the rest of Whosebourne was left alone — or at least, the creatures didn't get the chance to get to it before you saved us. And the town crafters are all pleased. They've got enough work on repairs to keep them busy and fed for months."

"Somebody's bad is somebody's good," Patience quoted a rare one of her mother's sayings that did *not* involve foxes. "How's your uncle?"

"He turned out to be quite fine. You were quite right about the fire just singeing him a touch. He's less brubarubaing these days, but that's not a bad thing. And he insisted we tend to you here at the house. Oh! And there's this!"

He set the one book on the bedside table and produced another from beneath his chair.

"*The Chaos Court*," Patience read aloud. "He gave it back."

"More than that." Linus wheezed in excitement. "He's letting it be published again. With *my* notes added in!"

"Good for you! That's the fattest goose at the fair and a gold-medal cheese all rolled into one!"

"Yes," said the Keyreeve from the doorway. "It would seem the old policy of secrets no longer served to keep the Chaos Court at bay. Mistakes were made. Orders were given that ought not, in hindsight, have been given. Things said and so forth."

Patience supposed that was the closest she was going to get to an apology. "Don't worry about it. Set your mind to do better tomorrow and you'll never know a night of sorrow."

"Brub. Quite."

He rocked back and forth on his heels for a minute, smiling his gassy-cow smile. Patience guessed he had something more to say but didn't know how to go on.

"The new place, sir?" Linus prompted.

"What? Oh, yes. Bruba. The place."

He cleared his throat. He spoke very officially. "Miss Patience Fell, in light of your service to the town and people of Whosebourne during our recent... bruba... unpleasantness... bruba... it is my privilege and pleasure as Keyreeve to offer you a place in service."

"I'm sure you have enough kitchen girls," Patience said. "Miss Alys needs me more, if it's all the same to you."

"It's not like that," Linus interjected.

"Bruba."

Linus explained. "My uncle wants to make you a special officer of the town. While the Fair Folk seem to have left, it is possible that a few stragglers might stick around to cause trouble. Or they could come back. Or there could be other stories come to life. Someone needs to care for things no one else is brave enough to face."

"Precisely. Well put, boy, well put. What this town needs is a Chief Broomguard. To deal with anything supersti — anything unnatur — anything otherwor — oh blast it, what's the word I'm looking for?"

"Foxbonnet odd?"

"Quite," the Keyreeve replied.

She didn't know what to say. An official position? With dangers unknown and weird creatures round every corner and her alone with only a cold iron broom to fight them all?

"It's a place that's perfect for you," Linus said. "Please? Won't you say yes?"

And, of course, she did.

## 41. One Must Still Be Brave

After the Keyreeve had left and she had shooed Linus out of her room—for the lovely little room on the second floor of Pennywhack Manor was *her* room now—Patience took a moment to look round her new home.

It was a room good enough for the fanciest guest. Her family would never believe she'd landed in a place so fine. Everything was so clean. An apple tree grew right outside the window, wafting in the smell of its fruit on the cool wind. She closed her eyes, just to stand and feel all that space that was hers.

Her iron broom hung in a place of honor over the fireplace. In the dresser were all her things, as well as more new clothes than she could imagine needing.

Moving around, she felt less stiff. She dressed, with a wince or two. She sat in a rocking chair by the window and thought about all she'd been through.

"No mistake, Patience Fell," she said to herself, "you did your job and did it well."

That reminded her of Mister Factotum. And the promise she'd made to him before he'd turned into pages. There was one more task she had to do.

She opened the door to the hall. Linus waited on a chair just outside, with a plate of cheese and bread and a glass of good, cold milk. Her stomach told her the last task could wait just a bit longer.

After she had eaten, she said, "I'd like to go visit Miss Crowquill, if I may."

"I anticipated that," Linus said. "I'll drive the fly myself."

Dusk gathered as they pulled up to *The Crock and Dice*. There was a sign out front:

ROOM AND FOOD FOR GIRL WITH BROOM

*inquire round the side*

Linus took the horse's head. He pulled a carrot from his pocket.

"You go ahead," he said. "I'll wait here."

Out of habit, Patience went round to the kitchen door. She stepped in a squishy bit of rain-soaked bread. Trash piled against the sides of the alley. A powerful stink filled the air. She smiled.

"Thank you very much, sir," she said with a curtsy.

The offaltosser poked his head out of a mold-swollen pumpkin. "Pike. Tweren't flippin nothin," he said, straining to contain his swears. "Never liked that schmecktenfrettle fox. Too fancy by far, with his snout in the air. Smelled bad too. All perfume and fake."

Patience knelt down in front of him. "How are your hands?"

He spread them out. They were quite dirty, but only had two small burn marks. "No lasting harm."

"I'm glad to hear it." She took one of his wee hands in both of hers and shook it. "You are kind and good."

The offaltosser swelled up with pride, nearly to burst. Unable to contain himself, he turned back into a funnel and blew off in a storm of trash and curses, down the alley and out of sight.

Inside, Miss Alys was stirring a pot of stew. She squinted at Patience.

"I don't see a broom," she said. "The sign says 'girl and broom'."

"I suppose," Patience said with a heavy fake sigh, "I'd better keep searching for a place."

"I heard you already had one."

Suddenly, Patience found herself seized by the cook. Stew spattered on her shoulder, but she didn't care. She hugged back hard as she could.

"You're a good broom girl," Miss Alys said. "The best there was."

She took a step back. She licked her thumb and scuffed a bit of stew off Patience's cheek. "If you ever get tired of fighting foxes and saving the world, we've got a life's worth of mess to clean up round here."

"I'll remember that. But for now—"

"Of course. Miss Crowquill, I'm guessing, is who you came to see. She's still up in her room, mad as the winds. But nothing, I reckon," the cook winked, "you can't handle."

The ladder to the attic waited for her.

Crowquill was sitting on her bed. Tears streamed from her eyes. She'd been blotting them with crumpled poem-papers. She blew her nose on her sleeve. When she saw Patience come up the hatch, she wailed.

"My poor Johnny!"

Patience put her arm around her. She let her weep great, jagged sobs of grief. Patience shed a quiet tear or two herself. Even though she hadn't known the old man, he'd been someone once, and now he was gone.

When Crowquill could cry no more, Patience let her go. She stood up. She put her hands on her hips.

"So, Miss Crowquill. You're on your own now."

"All on my own. For real and true."

"And what," Patience said, quoting Factotum, "are *you* going to do about it?"

"Wh-wh-what?"

A glob of snot quivered on the atticmad's upper lip. Patience wiped it off with a poem titled 'Atticmad's Sad Hymn to Him.'

"What. Are. *You*. Going to. Do?" She asked again.

"There's nothing I can do. I guess just wait here in the attic and send my poems out by crows who will n-n-h-h-e-ever come b-b-ack!"

In reply, Patience barked a word that would make an offaltosser blush. Crowquill's eyes got very wide.

"You, Miss Atticmad, are going to find your place in the world. Enough of this hiding under the roof and waiting for rescue. I promised Mister Factotum I'd roust you out, and roust you out I will."

Crowquill did not move.

Patience wasn't having any of it. "Do I have to get my broom?"

The atticmad stood up. "I-I can't. Don't you see? I'm not brave like you. There's no place in the world for me."

Patience snorted. "Oh please! *I'm* not brave like me."

Words tumbled out, just the right ones without her thinking. "I didn't just find my place in the world. Not like

I thought I would, anyway. Not like everyone says you're supposed to, just finding what's waiting for you.

"No. I found *a* place, and I made it mine. And when someone came along to make it a mess, I said 'no you don't' and I did something about it. And you will too."

"But—"

Patience prodded the other woman towards a water basin. "On you go. Wash your face. Out to the world to find your place."

From the window, moments later, Patience watched Crowquill stumble down the street with wandering steps and slow. Once the atticmad was out of sight, Patience rested her head on her arms. She gazed out over Whosebourne. Her place in the world. The rooftops were clear. Every cobble and trash-heap was where it should be. High up in the dusk's last light, crows circled on the whirling wind. Down below in the darkening streets, Linus waited to take her home.

Patience sighed and said, with some relief: "The. End."

*About the Writer*

**Jake Burnett** grew up on four continents and now lives in North Carolina with his wife, a one-eyed cat, and a very wiggly dog. *The Chaos Court* is his first novel. You can find out more about him at: http://www.jakeburnett.com/

## Preview: The Witch-Queen's Coven

"Are you a witch?"

"What?!" Patience's face got hot. "Why would you say that?"

"You carry a broom everywhere, don't you?"

The raggedy girl pushed her cap to the back of her head. She leaned against the toppled apple cart. She crunched a large and insolent bite out of a pilfered Fox Pippin.

Patience resisted the urge to whack her. "It's for my job."

"If you say so." The girl jabbed over Patience's shoulder with the scarlet-skinned fruit. "What about how you got that black bird? Following you. Like he's your what-you-witches-call-em. Familiar."

Sure enough, a crow strutted towards them across the market square. His black ruffed chest puffed up like one of the Keyreeve's boys about the town on official business. He brandished a scrap of paper in his beak.

"Familiar," Patience whispered…

*

*Whosebourne's squared away, but Miss Crowquill's gotten herself into a mess of trouble somewhere called Witsend. Patience Fell rides to the rescue and gets tangled in shenanigans that make fighting the Chaos Court look simple as sweeping the kitchen floor!*

Look for **The Witch-Queen's Coven**, coming in 2021 from South Window Press.

CPSIA information can be obtained
at www.ICGtesting.com
Printed in the USA
FSHW020459221220
76882FS